Caleb tried to remember a time when he had seen Anne wear a pair of jeans

He couldn't.

She always wore long, full dresses or skirts that came down to her ankles. Interesting.

A small smile graced her lips, and her ponytail bounced as she made her way toward him. Her fresh face and vivid blue eyes were a welcome sight. Anne never played games. After he had gotten past her shyness, he had found her very straightforward and honest. He could count on her if he ever needed help, especially with the kids from the youth center.

* * *

TINY BLESSINGS: Giving thanks for the neediest of God's children, and the families who take them in!

FOR THE TWINS' SAKE—
Jillian Hart (LI#308, July 2005)

BROUGHT TOGETHER BY BABY—
Carolyne Aarsen (LI#312, August 2005)

ON THE DOORSTEP—
Dana Corbit (LI#316, September 2005)

THE CINDERELLA PLAN—
Margaret Daley (LI#320, October 2005)

HER CHRISTMAS WISH—
Kathryn Springer (LI#324, November 2005)

PAST SECRETS, PRESENT LOVE—
Lois Richer (LI#328, December 2005)

Books by Margaret Daley

Love Inspired

The Power of Love #168
Family for Keeps #183
Sadie's Hero #191
The Courage To Dream #205
What the Heart Knows #236
A Family for Tory #245
**Gold in the Fire* #273
**A Mother for Cindy* #283
**Light in the Storm* #297
The Cinderella Plan #320

*The Ladies of Sweetwater Lake

MARGARET DALEY

feels she has been blessed. She has been married more than thirty years to her husband, Mike, whom she met in college. He is a terrific support and her best friend. They have one son, Shaun.

Margaret has been writing for many years and loves to tell a story. When she was a little girl, she would play with her dolls and make up stories about their lives. Now she writes these stories down. She especially enjoys weaving stories about families and how faith in God can sustain a person when things get tough. When she isn't writing, she is fortunate to be a teacher for students with special needs. Margaret has taught for over twenty years and loves working with her students. She has been a Special Olympics coach as well, and has participated in many sports with her students.

THE CINDERELLA PLAN

MARGARET DALEY

Published by Steeple Hill Books™

To the man I love, my husband, Mike.

Special thanks and acknowledgment are given to Margaret Daley for her contribution to the TINY BLESSINGS series.

STEEPLE HILL BOOKS

ISBN 0-373-81234-5

THE CINDERELLA PLAN

This edition published by arrangement with Steeple Hill Books.

www.SteepleHill.com

Printed in U.S.A.

Draw near to God,
and He will draw near to you.
—*James* 4:8

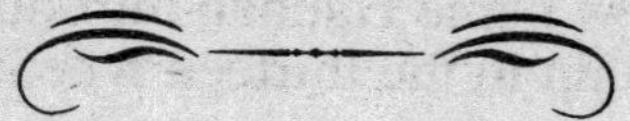

Caleb—Hebrew: Bold or dog; an Israelite who joined Moses from Egypt to live long enough to enter the Promised Land.

Anne—English: Graceful; a variant of the Hebrew name Hannah introduced to Britain in the thirteenth century.

Dylan—Welsh: Of the sea; In Welsh mythology, Dylan was the god of the sea. The Welsh name is from a different source than the Irish Dillon.

Chapter One

"Hey, Anne. Where's my crew?"

Standing on two telephone books stacked on a folding chair, Anne Smith gasped at the sudden sound of a deep baritone voice and lurched forward. She grasped the top of the bookshelf as the support beneath her feet teetered. Her fingers slipped from their precarious clasp on the wood while the chair crashed to the floor, its sound reverberating through the office. For a second she dangled from the bookcase before she lost her hold completely.

Strong arms enfolded her against a muscular chest, breaking her fall. Her heart beat frantically while she clutched Caleb Williams's shoulders to help steady both of them. They wobbled, as she had a few seconds ago, before Caleb managed to stabilize them.

A lopsided grin appeared on his face. "I don't usually have a woman fall for me."

Finding herself being held by Reverend Caleb Williams, not to mention his teasing comment, flustered Anne. Fantasies she didn't allow to surface taunted her thoughts of impossible dreams. Shoving them back into the dark recesses of her mind, she pulled away, smoothing back the few stray strands that had slipped from her ponytail. "I was concentrating on finding an old ledger. I didn't hear you opening the door."

"Can I help?"

Anne shook her head. "I was just going to look something up." She hated saying more with all that had happened lately at Tiny Blessings Adoption Agency.

Caleb peered at the metal folding chair lying on its side with the telephone books askew next to it. "That's no way to get something from the top shelf."

Heat scorched her cheeks. She knew better than to stack items on top of a chair, then use it like a ladder. But she had thought that maybe some of the old ledgers would have answers in them concerning the falsifying of adoption records. She would search the account books later. She wanted to help her employer, Kelly Young, with the mess the late director Barnaby Harcourt had left the agency in.

Caleb stepped over to the bookcase that went from the floor to the ceiling and pointed toward one of the account books kept on the top shelf. "Is that what you're looking for?"

"I'm not sure. I should probably look through them all."

He righted the chair and, without the telephone books, stood on it, easily reaching for the ledgers in question and handing them one by one to Anne, who stacked them on a table behind her desk. "There. Now I won't have to worry that you'll break your neck trying to get them down." He snared her with his intense blue eyes.

Anne's mouth went dry. She swallowed several times while backing up against the table where the old account books were. She needed to look away from Caleb, but for the life of her she couldn't. Today he was dressed casually in a pair of jeans and a long-sleeved light blue shirt that emphasized the vivid color of his eyes. He was the most handsome man she knew and was way off limits for her. He could date any woman he wanted in Chestnut Grove—for that matter, in the whole state of Virginia. She couldn't imagine he would be interested in her, and she'd best remember that. She tore her gaze from his and busied herself at restacking the ledgers until they were perfectly lined up—anything to keep her hands and mind off the man occupying her suddenly small office.

Caleb cleared his throat. "Where are the girls? I told them I would pick them up at four-thirty. I thought they would be outside waiting."

"They probably forgot the time. They're in the back conference room. They made some copies for me earlier and are stuffing envelopes. I gave them money for some soft drinks so they might be taking a break and forgot the time."

"You spoil them, Anne."

"They're a big help to me. I don't know if I could get everything done if it wasn't for the girls from the church's youth center volunteering here a couple of times a week."

"Keeps them busy and out of trouble."

"I can't see Gina, Tiffany or Nikki getting into trouble."

Caleb grinned, his whole face lit with a mischievous expression. "Teenager and trouble both start with the letter 't.' It wasn't that long ago you were one. Do you honestly feel that way?"

Thinking back to her days as a teenager

made her frown at the memories. They were not good ones. Hurt on top of hurt was what had characterized her formative years. But she doubted Caleb would understand what she had gone through, trying to fit in, trying to ignore the people who had made fun of her, trying to blend into the background so no one picked on her.

Anne forced a smile and said, "They have you to guide them."

Again Caleb snagged her gaze and held it. "And you. Tiffany has told me about your little talks."

"She has?"

"She has a crush on Billy and isn't sure what to do."

Anne hadn't been comfortable advising Tiffany on what to do about Billy because she could count on one hand how many dates she'd had as a teenager. But she had tried, thinking of the advice some of the magazines she'd read had given.

Caleb moved closer. "I like what you said about being yourself. It rarely works to change for another unless we really want that change, too."

Anne had nowhere to go, caught between the table and Caleb, so she straightened her shoulders, her arms stiff at her sides while clutching the wooden edge. "I'm glad Tiffany listened to me." She caught a whiff of his citrusy aftershave.

He plunged his fingers through his black hair, then rubbed his hand across the back of his neck, one corner of his mouth hiking into a wry grin. "Now *that* I'm not so sure about. She may have listened to what you said, but following your advice is a whole different matter. Tiffany's talking about having her mother take her shopping for dresses this weekend."

"Dresses? Tiffany? I never thought I would hear those two words said in the same sentence."

Moving back a step, Caleb half sat, half leaned against Anne's desk, his arms folded across his chest. "Yeah, she's quite a little tomboy, but she wants to impress Billy, and she thinks wearing dresses will do it."

Relieved to have a little breathing room, Anne relaxed the tense set of her shoulders. "Who told her that?"

"Nikki."

"Oh, this should be interesting. Has Nikki talked Tiffany into buying some black dresses?"

Caleb chuckled. "Your crew of workers is quite diverse, I must say."

Anne lounged against the table, trying her best not to allow Caleb's presence in her office to throw her off-kilter too much—if that were even possible. "Let's see. Nikki only wears black and listens to punk rock in her spare time. Tiffany is a tomboy through and through, and Gina is our resident genius. Yes, I would say you're right, but technically they're *your* crew. You recruited them, and bring them here and pick them up."

"But only you, Anne, have made these three girls work as a team. Now at the church youth center they hang out together. Six months ago they wouldn't have been caught in the same room because of their differences."

Anne hadn't thought her cheeks could redden anymore than they had earlier when she had been caught against his chest, but if the singeing heat was any indication, her face was beet red, especially with Caleb staring at her. She hated to think what he saw through his eyes when looking at her. A plain Jane, someone who had learned to fade into the background. If someone would make office camouflage, she would wear it.

"Is that why you had them work together?" Anne managed to ask, desperate to keep the conversation centered on the girls, not her.

"Ah, you've discovered my strategy. Let's hope they don't." He pushed away from the desk. "I guess I'd better round up the girls. It's a school night, and I'm sure they'll have homework to do." Starting for the door, he flicked a glance toward Anne. "I realize you don't get the church newsletter so you might not know all the details concerning the upcoming carnival. Would you like to help this year?"

"Sure."

"Have the girls said anything to you about the fall carnival for the youth center?"

One stray strand of her hair tickled her cheek. She brushed it back, hooking it behind her ear. "No. What were they supposed to say?"

"More like ask." He flashed her a grin. "I'll let them break the news to you."

His devastating smile momentarily drew her attention away from what he'd said. Then his words sank in. "Break the news? That doesn't sound good." Anne followed Caleb from her office and fell into step beside him as they walked down the hall, which was lined with photos of children and their adoptive families, to the conference room where the girls were working.

"I suppose it will depend on how adventurous you are."

"There isn't an adventurous bone in my body."

His gaze skimmed down the length of her. "Not even one?" One brow quirked upward.

She shook her head, unable to say a thing when he was looking at her so intently with a gleam in his blue eyes. His classic good looks and charm did strange things to her stomach, causing it to churn with emotions she wished she could control. Thinking of him in any light other than as a casual friend would only hurt her in the end.

"I seem to remember that at the last fall carnival you manned the booth where anyone with a buck could throw a pie at you."

"That wasn't adventurous."

"I thought you were a brave soul."

"Nah. I love pies, especially the ones from the Starlight Diner. So I made some money for the center and got to taste some delicious pies in the meantime. Nothing adventurous in that." She reached out to stop him before entering the conference room, her hand immediately falling to her side when she realized what she'd done. Her fingertips tingled from the brief contact. "What have they cooked up this year for the adults? I don't like surprises." Lack of control in her youth had firmed that in her mind. She worked hard to keep control in her life as much as possible.

"Oh, something magnificent, you could say." He winked at her, then shoved open the door and stepped into the room.

The sound of the young girls' laughter filled the air, then several "be quiets" when they realized Caleb and Anne were coming into the room.

"Okay, I can tell a conspiracy when I confront one. What are you three up to?" Although Caleb planted his hand on his waist and stared at each one of the young girls, an impish glint danced in his eyes while one side of his mouth twitched from suppressing a smile.

Tiffany peered at Gina for a long moment, her lips clamped together while she tried to contain her own smile. Nikki dropped her head until her chin almost touched her chest, her concentration focused totally on her lap. Anne got the feeling she was the only one not in on a big secret.

Gina shifted in her chair and said, "We were wondering what was taking you so long. Now we know." The fifteen-year-old pointedly looked at Caleb, then slid her attention to Anne.

She felt like pushing the girls out of the

way and hiding under the large round table they sat at. She knew she and Caleb had been the topic of conversation only seconds before he'd opened the door. What were they planning? The expression in the young girls' eyes warned Anne to be wary.

Gina stood, stretching and twisting. "I'm glad you're here, Anne. We want to make sure you're coming to the fund-raiser for the youth center."

"Sure. I do every year."

Tiffany sighed. "Good. That's what Gina said."

Anne stepped back, her hand behind her clasping the doorknob—just in case she needed to make a fast getaway. Something was brewing in the air and she was sure she was involved somehow—probably not to her liking. "Do you want me to man the pie-throwing booth again this year?"

Gina shook her head. "No, that would mess up your costume."

"Costume?" The word nearly choked in her throat, her hand tightening around the knob.

Caleb swung around and faced her. "The youth committee working on the fund-raiser decided this year to charge a flat fee for the event and have all the adults dress up in costumes representing their favorite fairy-tale characters. There'll be an article in the newspaper tomorrow."

"I dressed in a costume for the article," Gina said, shoving her chair toward the table. "We're even going to provide costumes for people who need them. Nikki's aunt in Richmond owns a party store with lots of costumes she's going to let us have for the day."

That didn't seem too bad. Anne relaxed her death-hold on the knob.

Dressed all in black, Nikki lifted her head. "Yeah, there's even gonna be prizes—for the best couple, the funniest and the scariest costumes. The kids are gonna be the judges."

"What made you decide to do costumes this year?" Anne released her grip on the knob and moved forward.

"Adults don't play enough. We wanted to turn the tables around and run the booths, but we aren't charging for each activity like we have in the past. Fun is the theme for the night." Gina gathered up the envelopes they had been stuffing and placed them into a box.

"It sounds like you've got things under control. But if you need any help, I'll be glad to." Anne took the box from Gina.

"That's great. We could use your help. Time's running out."

Anne noticed the surprised expression on Caleb's face and wondered about it, but before she could ask him, Gina continued, "This weekend we're gonna make flyers at the center, then put them up all over town to remind everyone about the annual event one last time."

"I'll be there. What time?"

"Early. Eight."

Anne smiled. For someone who usually got up at five every morning, eight wasn't early. "Eight it is."

"Let's go, kids. We need to meet with the rest of the committee at the center in fifteen minutes. Reverend Fraser and his wife will be waiting for us." Caleb stood to the side as the three teenage girls hurried out of the open door and down the hall.

"They seem eager about the carnival. That's great to see." Anne again found herself alone with Caleb and tension, held at bay while the room was full with three teenagers, came rushing back.

"Yeah, I'm letting the kids have a bigger role in the carnival this year. Gina came to me and asked. Since the fund-raiser is all about them, it seemed a logical decision at the time, but the carnival is only ten days away."

"And there's still so much to do?"

He nodded. "Coming up with what they wanted to do took longer than I had planned, or I would have started this back at the beginning of summer rather than the end."

"It's an annual event. The important thing about the fall carnival isn't what you do, but that the proceeds go for the church youth center and the kids who use it. Everyone knows about the carnival and has probably already made plans to attend. It's always been the second weekend in October. I can help with more than the flyers if you need me to."

"Could you? Gina, Tiffany and Nikki really respond to you. This year the committee agreed that this would be a children's production with minimal oversight from us adults. But if Gina has invited you to help with the flyers, maybe you could also help with the decorating of the hall. You were the first adult outside the committee she has asked to help with the preparations."

"Then I'll see if I can wrangle an invite from her when I'm helping them on Saturday."

Relief erased the tension in his expression. "Thank you. You're a lifesaver. I haven't been sleeping like I should, worrying about this fund-raiser."

The urge to comfort him inundated her. She balled her hands at her sides to keep from touching his arm, to assure him everything would work out. "It's good to see them so involved in something that directly affects them. The youth center is all about them. They will be the ones using the new rec equipment you'll purchase with the money raised."

"I know, and I really do think it's a terrific idea that they're so involved with the carnival, but I keep telling Gina that's what I get paid the big bucks for—to worry."

"So much of what has to be done are last-minute things. It'll all come together."

"If not, I guess I could always stand on the corner with a tin cup in whatever costume the kids pick out for me to wear and beg for the money."

Anne chuckled. She loved the way Caleb could laugh at himself. His air of confidence drew her to him. She wished she felt that way about herself. "Mmm." She tapped her finger against her chin. "There are all kinds of possibilities for your costume. There's the Papa Bear from *Goldilocks and the Three Bears.* Then there's the Big Bad Wolf from *Little Red Riding Hood.* Either one would be interesting to see."

"Yeah, I'm afraid it might be. I'm just worried about wearing tights." Grinning, he headed into the hall and started for the front door.

Anne walked with him to the entrance, then watched him make his way to his white Suburban. She waved goodbye to him and the girls, hoping none of the longing she felt deep inside revealed itself. Even though she wasn't involved at the church where he was a youth minister, she did volunteer some of her time at the youth center connected to the Chestnut Grove Community Church. She'd toyed with the idea of going to the church on Sunday, but she'd never attended services while growing up, except when she was a young girl and had gone to visit Grandma Rose. Caleb made her wonder what she was missing. Sighing, Anne turned away from the door and walked back toward her office, where she could disappear into her quiet refuge and pour through those old ledgers.

Tucking her white buttoned-down shirt into her stiff, dark blue jeans, Anne stood in front of her mirror that was mounted on the back of her bedroom door. A frown drew her brows together as she assessed herself. With her blond hair pulled back into a tight ponytail that hung down below her shoulder blades and her face scrubbed clean, all she could think of to describe herself was plain, dull.

Normally that didn't bother her. But maybe she should wear a touch of lipstick or eye shadow to bring out the blue in her eyes? She turned her head from side to side, trying to decide what to do. She would be working in the same room with Caleb today for *hours.*

She rubbed her sweaty palms down her brand-new pair of jeans. She should have washed them. They looked new—too blue. But she hadn't had any time because she'd only bought the jeans on impulse last night when she'd realized she had nothing to wear that didn't make her seem much older than her twenty-nine years.

Why hadn't she also bought that red scarf to tie in her hair? Because she didn't wear any colors that made her stand out in a crowd. She didn't want to attract attention. She'd had more than her share while growing up—the unwanted kind.

Her gaze strayed until it lit upon her black leather shoes by her queen-size bed that had a huge fluffy counterpane in different shades of pink. At least her shoes weren't as bad as the ones she had worn in elementary and high school. She shuddered thinking about those therapeutic ones, necessary because she was so severely pigeon-toed.

Who was she kidding? She didn't want to stand out today either. She was better off in the background, going through life unnoticed. So Caleb would be at the youth center. That didn't mean they would spend any alone-time together. That didn't even mean they would talk much. There were going to be a lot of kids at the center. She was going to be there to help make flyers for the carnival. That was all.

Anne spun away from her image in the mirror, irritated at herself for even going out and buying a pair of jeans. As if that would make a difference. How could a man like Caleb ever be interested in her? He was handsome, outgoing, so self assured—everything she wasn't.

"Anne, you need to stop dreaming the impossible," she muttered and sat on her bed to slip on her brand-new pair of corrective shoes that she'd saved six months for. The black leather would go with most of her clothes and the pair was certainly more stylish than the ones before. She wished she could afford several different colors and styles, but on her limited budget, even living with her parents, this was it.

* * *

Caleb sat on the front steps leading into the youth center housed in the church hall next to the Chestnut Grove Community Church. Nursing a large mug of coffee cupped between his hands, he took a few minutes to sort through his thoughts before the long day started. Weather permitting, he enjoyed doing this every morning.

Lord, I hope I don't regret allowing the children to organize and oversee this fund-raiser. I'm getting anxious. We only have a week till the carnival and there's still so much to do. Gina assures me she and her friends have everything under control. But still—the center needs the rec equipment.

He took a large swallow of his lukewarm coffee, looking toward the church next door. Its white and red bricks gleamed in the sun, just peeking over the tops of the oak and maple trees along the street. The tall spire and bell tower of the eighteenth-century structure shot up into the blue sky as though it stood sentinel over the town. When peering at the church that had withstood centuries amid war and drama, he always felt comforted. The Lord's house. An intricate part of Chestnut Grove and its history.

A small black car pulled into the parking

lot at the side of the center, capturing his attention. He watched as Anne climbed from her old Chevy and headed up the sidewalk toward him. Tilting his head to the left, he tried to remember a time when he had seen her wear a pair of jeans. He couldn't. She always wore long, full dresses or skirts that came down to her ankles. Interesting.

A small smile graced her lips and her ponytail bounced as she made her way toward him. Her fresh face and vivid blue eyes were a welcome sight. Anne never played games. After he had gotten past her shyness, he had found her very straightforward and honest. He could count on her if he ever needed help, especially with the young people who volunteered at the adoption agency. Anne took them under her wing and assisted them any way possible. She was a very caring woman. An appealing quality. If only she believed in God, he thought, pushing to his feet and plastering a smile of greeting on his face.

"You're here before the kids are." He checked his watch. "In fact, you're ten minutes early before eight on a Saturday. I'm impressed."

"Mornings are the best time of day. I've never slept past six-thirty."

He held up his mug. "Whereas, I have to load up on tons of coffee, just to be coherent before nine in the morning."

"So you're a night person?"

"No, more like an afternoon person. My best time is between one and five."

She laughed. "I'll have to remember that."

He liked the sound of her laughter, light, almost musical. It sent a warmth through him that surprised him. "Do you want some coffee before the kids swarm this place and there isn't a moment's rest?"

"I'm a tea drinker."

"Something else we don't agree on."

She shrugged. "Yep. Coffee tastes like dirt to me."

"To me drinking tea is like drinking brownish water."

Anne started climbing the stairs toward the front door. "The world would be a dull place if we all agreed on everything."

Caleb walked next to her. "I have to agree with you on that."

She slanted a look toward him, grinning. "I guess we aren't so hopeless after all. Who knows what else we might agree on before the day is out?"

"Let me refill my coffee. I'll meet you in the arts-and-crafts room. That's where I thought we would make the flyers and go over any last minute preparations."

While Anne headed to the left, Caleb walked toward the kitchen connected to the cafeteria/gym. With a lightness to his step, he hurried to pour his coffee and get back to Anne. He had known her from a distance for a few years, but in the past six months he had become better acquainted with her. Each time he was with her he felt her emotional walls crumble just a little more. The minister and psychologist in him wanted to help her heal, because in her blue eyes he saw a glimpse of a deep wound she tried to conceal from the world. Maybe in helping her heal, he could also help her find her way to the Lord.

But lately, the man in him wanted something more. That continued to surprise him because he wasn't interested in dating anyone who didn't believe in the Lord. He'd had a relationship in college with a woman who had not been a Christian and the emotional scars left from it still hurt today. He'd wanted it to work so badly, but they just hadn't seen the future the same way.

He eased open the door to the arts-and-crafts room, expecting to find Anne waiting for him. His words died in his throat as he scanned the area before him. The emptiness mocked him. He glanced up and down the hall, wondering where she was. Then he heard a noise and looked back into the room. He saw Anne, on all fours, scooting out from under one of the long art tables.

He cleared his throat. "Can I help?"

Anne gasped, lifted up and bumped into the underside of the table. "Ouch!" She managed to stand without injuring herself again, but she rubbed the back of her head. "You're supposed to warn someone you're in the room."

"Sorry. I did. I cleared my throat. But next time I'll clap my hands or bang on something so you know I'm coming." Caleb put his mug down. "May I ask why you were under the table in the first place?"

"I was putting away my car keys and I dropped my purse." She gestured toward the floor on the other side of the table, away from the door. "My lipstick rolled there."

"You don't need makeup."

With his gaze fixed on her face, she blushed the color of her pink lipstick and busied herself stuffing the contents of her purse back into the black leather bag.

"You don't carry much. My two cousins have half their bedroom in their purses."

She shrugged, snapping the bag closed

with a loud click. "Don't need it. I don't wear much makeup. That is, other than lipstick. Personally, I wish I didn't have to carry a purse at all, but I need something to put my wallet and checkbook in."

"Very efficient."

Her smile encompassed her whole face, two dimples appearing. "That's my middle name."

"Very or efficient?" he asked, pressing his lips together to keep from laughing.

She chuckled. "Efficient and organized."

He could listen to her laughter all day. What a beautiful sound! He would have to think of more ways to get her to do it. "I'm glad you're both because we'll probably need it when the kids arrive. The last meeting we had ended in chaos. Gina wanted to do things a certain way and Jeremy another way. Needless to say, that didn't sit well with Gina. She's very aware he's the oldest by a year."

Anne peered at the clock on the wall. "Where are they?"

"You know, that's a good question." Caleb started for the door.

Jeremy appeared in the entrance into the room, a frown slashing across his face. "I went to pick up Dylan like I promised ya and he's gone."

"What do you mean gone?" Caleb straightened, anxiety taking hold of him.

"His foster parents went to get him in his room, and he hadn't slept in his bed. He wasn't anywhere in the house. They called the police, but I thought ya should know."

Chapter Two

Anne came to stand beside Caleb. "Dylan? Isn't that the boy the Givens family took in?"

Caleb nodded, thinking back to his conversation with the child yesterday afternoon—or the lack thereof. Dylan had been unusually quiet when Caleb had seen him at the center, staring at the TV set. He suspected the eleven-year-old hadn't even known what show had been on. He'd tried to get Dylan to talk to him, but the boy had clamped his mouth shut, crossed his arms and glared at a spot on the floor in front of him.

Caleb dug into his pocket and retrieved his car keys. "I need to find him." He started for the door.

"Do you want me to help?" Anne asked, taking a step forward.

He pivoted, a frown creasing his forehead. “No.”

The force behind that one word stiffened her spine.

“Sorry. That didn’t come out right.” Caleb kneaded the back of his neck. “I need you to stay here and get the kids started on the flyers. I hope I can find Dylan and be back soon.”

“What if he shows up here? Do you have a cell phone I can call you on?”

With a quick nod Caleb walked back to the table and scribbled his number down on a pad. “Call if you find out anything that might help.”

As Caleb left the room, Jeremy stood near the door, looking lost. An uncomfortable silence descended. Anne shifted from one foot to the other, not sure what to do. She knew from the girls who volunteered at the adoption agency that Jeremy was very popular at school, already a star athlete on the football team even though he was only a sophomore. When Gina talked about him, she got all starry-eyed, and Anne thought back to her days in high school and the few crushes she’d developed on unattainable boys. It hadn’t taken long for them to be crushed to the point she didn’t dream about the impossible—until Caleb had come along.

Anne coughed and swallowed several

times to coat her dry throat. "I'm sure that Caleb will find Dylan."

Jeremy finally looked at her as though he hadn't realized she'd even been in the room, which was usually how Anne liked it. But his expression only heightened all the years that she had felt invisible, unimportant.

The teenager lifted his shoulders. "Yeah, I guess so. I should've known something was up. The last few days he didn't dog my every step around here like he usually does."

"Oh" was all Anne could think to say. She'd never had very good success talking with the opposite sex and even though she was almost twice Jeremy's age, she wasn't doing a good job at the moment.

Luckily Gina burst into the room, followed by Nikki, Tiffany and Ruth Fraser, the minister's daughter, all of them talking at the same time. Gina took one look at Jeremy and slowed her pace, her words dying in her throat as she quickly peered away from the young man.

When Gina saw Anne, the fifteen-year-old said, "I'm glad you could make it." Then, as though she realized something was wrong, she cocked her head and asked, "What happened?"

"Dylan ran away," Jeremy answered before Anne could even open her mouth.

Gina glanced at Jeremy, her usual bravado subdued. "He did? When?"

"Last night, I guess."

The girls behind Gina began to whisper among themselves. Anne stepped forward. "If you all know anything, please tell me. Caleb is out looking for Dylan right now. Do you know where he would go when he's upset?"

Tiffany and Nikki shook their heads. Ruth stared at a spot on the far wall with a blank expression, none of her usual exuberance evident.

Anne walked to her. "Do you know something, Ruth?"

The girl's shoulders drooped, her bright red hair falling forward, almost concealing her face.

"Please tell me."

Ruth looked Anne in the eye. "Dylan wasn't happy with his foster family. He's been talking about leaving, but I didn't think he would do it."

"Do you know where he would go?"

Ruth bit her lower lip, shaking her head slowly. "He went to school and here. Those are the only places he went to."

An idea popped into Anne's mind. They hadn't searched the center. "Is this all the committee?"

"No, there are a few more. Billy is always late and Tyler is always with him," Gina answered.

"Why don't you get everyone started, Gina. I'll be right back."

Anne quickly left the committee working on the flyers and began searching each room, hoping her hunch paid off. When she entered the TV room, she spotted Dylan curled up on the old chocolate brown couch, hugging a plaid pillow. His black hair was tousled, his clothes twisting about him as though he had wrestled all night. She scanned the area, wondering how he'd gotten into the center. An opened window answered her question, and a breeze blew the white curtains, bringing the scent of the outdoors inside along with the early morning chill.

Anne walked to the window and closed it, then locked it. There wasn't a lot of crime in Chestnut Grove, but leaving a window unlocked probably wasn't a wise decision. She would say something to Caleb when he returned.

Dylan stirred on the couch, rolling onto his back. One arm flopped over the edge, dangling almost to the wooden floor. Even in sleep his face tensed into a frown, deep lines marring his forehead.

Anne gently shook Dylan awake. The boy's blue eyes flew open. He scrambled to a sitting position.

"You've got some people worried about you." Anne sat down on the worn coffee table in front of the couch.

Dylan stuck out his lower lip and clutched the pillow even tighter to his chest, his brows drawn together.

"Are you okay?"

His pout strengthened into a scowl. "Yeah."

"I need to call Caleb and let him know you're here. He's out looking for you."

"He is?"

Anne nodded, wishing she could wrap her arms around the boy and comfort him. His eyes reflected his doubt and pain. At a young age she sensed Dylan had seen the rough side of life and was having a hard time coping with it.

She stood. "Everyone's in the arts-and-crafts room working on the flyers. Why don't you join them? They'll be glad to know you're okay."

For a long moment Dylan remained on the couch, staring straight ahead, grasping the pillow against him, as though it were his shield against the world, making a mockery of his declaration that he was all right. When Anne started forward, he tossed the pillow aside, unfolded himself and rose in one quick motion. He fled out the door.

Anne hurried after him, afraid that he was leaving. When he disappeared into the arts-and-crafts room, she came to a halt in the hallway and listened for a moment to the others greeting Dylan. Taking a quivering breath, Anne used the phone near the front entrance to call Caleb.

Hearing Caleb's deep baritone voice made her momentarily forget why she wanted to talk to him. Silence ruled for a few seconds as she pictured him in her mind—over six feet tall, a large, muscular chest and narrow waist as though he used the exercise equipment at the center regularly, straight black hair that brushed his collar and light blue eyes that sparkled with humor.

"Anne? Did you find him?"

"How did you know it was me?" she asked, surprised and embarrassed at the same time.

"Caller ID. Did you find Dylan?"

"Yes. He's at the youth center. I think he's been here all night, in the TV room."

"I'll be right there. Don't let him leave."

"Do you want me to call the Givens' and the police?"

"No, I'll take care of it. Thanks, Anne. I didn't think to look around the center before leaving. You saved us all a lot of time."

The warmth in his words colored her cheeks, making her realize it didn't take much to please her when it came to Caleb. She was a pushover where that man was concerned. Thankfully he didn't know the power he had over her. She would hate to see pity in his eyes.

When Anne reentered the arts-and-crafts room, everyone was busy making flyers under Gina's directions. The girl motioned for her to come closer. She and Gina had always been on friendly terms while the teenager volunteered at Tiny Blessings, but Anne was still surprised by the invitation to help, especially when it seemed Gina had everything under control. She sat beside the young girl who slid a piece of white paper toward her.

Gina showed Anne another slip of paper. "This is what we want on each of the flyers. Other than that, you can get as creative as you want to draw people's eyes to the flyer."

"Poster" was a more accurate word for what she was going to make, Anne thought as she looked at the large blank paper before her. Creative? She didn't have a creative bone in her body, even though she loved to paint in her free time, just for herself. When she painted, she let her emotions fill the blank canvas. Knowing no one would see her work made it easy to do whatever she felt at the moment. A poster to be put up all around town was different.

Anne sighed heavily and plunged into the work before her. There was nothing wrong with plain and simple, she decided as she began to print the necessary information on the poster. She wasn't so engrossed in her work that she didn't know the second that Caleb entered the room. The hairs on the nape of her neck tingled and a shiver went down her spine. He came immediately over to where she was. Her hand shook as she wrote the last letter and thankfully put the marker down before her reaction became obvious to anyone.

"May I have a word with you in private?" Caleb whispered into her ear.

His breath fanned her neck, heightening the chills she already had from his entrance. She nodded, afraid to say anything for fear her voice would betray her.

He stepped back while she scooted her chair away from the long table and rose. She followed him out into the hall.

"I didn't want to say anything to Dylan

until I talked to you first. Did he tell you why he ran away?"

"No. I didn't want to frighten him by asking him too many questions. A window in the TV room was open. I think he used it to climb into the building."

Caleb frowned. "They're usually locked. Dylan was the last one to leave the room yesterday. I wonder if he unlocked it. If he did, that means he was planning to run away."

"But why here?"

"That's a good question, and one I mean to ask Dylan. Will you continue to help the others while I have a word with him?"

"Sure. Are the Givens' coming to pick him up?"

"No, I told them I would bring him home later after I talk with him."

"I—" Anne started to say something, then clamped her mouth shut.

"What?"

"Nothing. It's none of my business."

"If it's about Dylan, it is. You found him. What did you want to tell me."

"I've known the Givens family for most of my life. They take in foster children as a way to make a living. They feed, clothe and take care of their basic needs, but they're not what I would call real parents. Right now they have several children and I wonder if Dylan is getting lost in the crowd there. How long has Dylan been with them?"

"Not long, a little over a month, I believe. I've been trying to counsel him, but he hasn't opened up."

"But he comes to the center?"

"Every day after school."

"Then you must be reaching him on some level or he wouldn't spend so much time here. And when he ran away, he came here."

He took her hand. The gesture surprised Anne. His warm grasp enclosed about her fingers, underscoring all her dreams where this man was concerned. If she was anyone but who she was, she might have a chance—

"Will you come with me when I take Dylan home? Maybe another pair of eyes will help me understand how to help him, how to assess the dynamics of the family."

He was holding her hand. There wasn't anyway she could deny him his request even though she felt inadequate to assess the dynamics of any family, especially when she thought of her own parents who were so wrapped up in their careers they never had time for her. She choked out, "Yes," then swallowed several times before adding, "I'll try, but counseling is your area of expertise, not mine."

He squeezed her hand and smiled at her. "Thank you. I knew I could count on you, Anne. And don't sell yourself short. Tiffany, Nikki and Gina rave about you."

Her world tilted and spun. Through a supreme effort she managed not to collapse at his feet. "They do?"

"You know those little talks you have over sodas?"

She waved her free hand, her senses still fixated on the fact he held her hand. "That's just girl talk."

"Well, you must be saying something right, Anne. They're listening, and that's most of the battle with kids."

You are not going to blush like a school girl, she ordered herself, removing her hand from his and stepping back to give herself some breathing room. Her lungs burned from lack of proper oxygen, and she still felt dangerously close to fainting in front of him. She quickly realized, however, that she needed more space than a few measly feet. His presence dominated the hallway.

"I thought you two were gonna help us with the flyers," Gina said from the doorway of the arts-and-crafts room, a twinkle glittering in her eyes.

Anne bit down on her lower lip and hurried forward, past the girl into the room. If the heat from her face was any indication, she was sure her cheeks were five different shades of red. She wished she didn't blush at the least little thing. She slipped into the chair she'd occupied and picked up a red marker, using it to outline the black lettering she'd done earlier. The words stood out against the white poster board.

"That's great, Anne. I like it. Your lettering is beautiful. Don't you think so, Caleb?" Gina grinned at her as she sat down next to her and began decorating her own flyer.

Anne kept her focus trained on her paper, but she heard Caleb's words as he took up the chair across from her. "Maybe we should have Anne do all the lettering. It sure beats my printing."

"Yeah, that's not a bad idea. What do you think, guys?"

Before Anne realized it she had all the poster boards stacked in front of her to print the information on. She was perfectly happy to do it, because beyond the outlining of the words, she had been clueless with what she'd wanted to do next to her flyer. This way she could do what she did best and let the others be creative.

Pleased at how the morning had turned out,

she glanced up to find Caleb staring at her with an intense expression on his face. She should look away, but for the life of her, she couldn't make herself avert her gaze. She liked looking at Caleb, not just because he was handsome, which he definitely was, but because he was so kind and caring. For a blissful moment the others were forgotten, the rest of the world fading from her awareness as their gazes connected across the table and she felt his pull, strong, compelling—and dangerous to her quiet, uneventful life.

Caleb pulled up to the curb outside the Givens' large two story white house with Dylan sitting between him and Anne. The frown on the boy's face grew deeper the nearer they'd come to his foster home, but Dylan remained staunchly quiet even though Anne had tried to engage him in conversation.

Caleb was aware Dylan, who had lived in Richmond, had been recently taken away from his father because of abandonment. Was there more to the story than the child's father leaving Dylan while the man was on a drinking binge? Glancing at the boy's angry expression brought back memories Caleb wished would stay buried. His hands about the steering wheel tightened as he fought against the onslaught of emotions that he usually kept reined in. Helplessness. Anger for his childhood friend. Despair.

Please, Lord, I need Your help with Dylan. How do I reach him? I've tried for the past month. He's angry and keeping things bottled up. Show me the way.

Rex Givens stood on the porch waiting for them as they walked up to the house. One small child played off to the side with some trucks while a toddler, dressed in a diaper and a long-sleeved blue pullover shirt, pressed his face against the screen door.

Caleb extended his hand toward Rex. "It's good to see you. As you can see, Dylan's okay."

Rex snorted, fastening his full attention on the boy. "We were worried sick about you. What did you think running away would prove?"

Dylan's frown evolved into a scowl, deep grooves at the sides of his mouth. Silent, he stared at Rex, his chin hiked up a notch.

The man gestured toward the six-year-old on the porch. "Take Brent inside and tell Cora you're home."

Dylan stomped up the stairs, but when he spoke to Brent, none of the boy's anger showed in his tone of voice as he helped the younger boy gather up his trucks. They disappeared inside the house, Dylan taking hold of the toddler's hand as they ambled down the hallway.

Anne moved closer to Caleb, filling the void Dylan's absence created. A strong urge to reach out and grasp her hand for support inundated Caleb as he'd waited for the children to leave. His palms tingled as though an electrical current passed through him.

"May we have a word, Rex?" Caleb finished mounting the remaining two steps, not intending to be put off by the man.

Rex backed up, then waved his arms toward a grouping of white wicker furniture at one end of the porch. "Fine. Dinner will be soon and I'll need to wash up. It's quite a chore getting five children all to sit down at the table and eat at the same time."

"This won't take long. I'm concerned about Dylan, as I'm sure you are. Thankfully, Anne found him before he decided to leave the center." Caleb's gaze slid to Anne, and her presence next to him soothed some of the tension festering in him. Her sweet, caring attitude reminded him of what was good in life.

Rex sat in the lone wicker chair, leaving the small love seat for Caleb and Anne. As he lowered himself next to her, again the desire to touch her for support made him falter, and his mind went blank for a few seconds. Silence reigned while he grappled with his feelings, ones he hadn't had in a long while.

Rex cleared his throat. "The only thing I can think that set Dylan off last night was he didn't get to see a TV show he had wanted to. With five children in the house, he has his chores that have to be done and he wasn't through with the dishes when the show came on."

"I understand." Caleb forced himself to keep his hands from clenching at his sides. Chores were an important part of a family, but, like Anne, he wasn't so sure about the Givens' motives for taking in foster children. He'd been around other foster parents, especially Reverend Fraser and his wife, who loved their charges and their home reflected that love. When he'd been inside the Givens' home, he didn't feel that kind of love for the children. They were a business to Rex and Cora Givens. "I'd like to counsel Dylan on a formal basis. He needs more than he's getting right now coming to the center and just hanging out."

Rex straightened his large frame in the small chair, its creaking sound permeating the porch. "You can say that again. Dylan's more than Cora and me can handle. He resents any work we want him to do around the house. His attitude has been affecting the others in the short time he's been here." He crossed his arms. "Frankly, we don't know what to do about the boy anymore. We're thinking of calling the state to place him somewhere else."

Caleb's hand curled into a fist. "Let me work with him first. Give me a chance."

"He's been going to the youth center for the past month and nothing about his attitude has changed."

"It takes time, Mr. Givens," Anne said, shifting next to Caleb, her hand brushing up next to his fist, as though she sensed his tension and was trying to reassure him.

Her soft voice tempered Caleb, and he uncurled his hand. *Lord, what do I do? Dylan needs me.*

"I can't let the boy disrupt my household and set the wrong example. I have four other children to think about."

Caleb didn't want Dylan to be moved from foster home to foster home if there was a better solution. "Give me until the end of this month before you make a decision. Please." He gave up fighting his feelings and took

Anne's hand. Out of the corner of his eye he saw her surprise reflected in her expression, but he didn't release his hold nor did she pull her hand away.

Rex rose. "Fine. But if things don't get better soon, I'll be talking to Dylan's case manager about another foster home."

Caleb stood at the same time as Anne, their clasped hands dropping to their sides. For a second he had a strong urge to grab hold of her again. Stunned by the need, he stepped away. "Don't say anything to Dylan about your plans."

"You've got four weeks, Reverend. Things have got to get better or Dylan needs to go back to the state."

Anne stiffened and started to say something but stopped herself. Instead, she stalked down the steps and walked toward his Suburban. Caleb watched her until she stopped at the curb and waited for him. He, too, fought the anger roiling in his stomach. Rex Givens wanted only easy children to raise. Life wasn't that simple. Caleb wondered how much of the man's attitude Dylan was aware of.

"What's *her* problem?" Rex asked, tossing his head in the direction of Anne.

Caleb bit back what he really wanted to

say to the man about children being precious resources, not commodities to trade in when something didn't go just right. He needed a chance to counsel Dylan and that meant going through Rex Givens. "I'll start working with Dylan after school on Monday if that's okay with you," he said, rather than answering Rex.

"Fine." The large man shuffled toward the screen door. "Personally I think it's a waste of your time. But then it's your time, not mine."

Caleb hurried from the porch before he said something he shouldn't. Anne leaned against his car, her ankles crossed, her arms folded over her chest, nothing casual about her stance. When she lifted her gaze to his, all the anger he felt was deep in her eyes. He reached around her and opened the door. She slipped inside.

When he slid in behind the wheel, the swirling tension in the small confines of his Suburban escalated to a minitornado. He twisted around to look at her and try to defuse the moment.

"I can't believe that man! Did you hear him? Those children don't mean a thing to him. I know foster parents aren't always easy to find, but he and Cora shouldn't be ones at all. I—" Her mouth closed about the words she was going to say, the line of her jaw hard.

Anne's face in her self-righteous anger was a beautiful sight to behold. She was like a female bear protecting her cubs, intending to throw her body in the way of danger. The zeal in Anne appealed to him. Why had he never seen it before? Because she was a master at keeping herself in the background, of blending in so no one noticed her. But he noticed her now—the flushed cheeks, the blue sparkle in her eyes, the full pouty lips.

"I know. I wish I had an—" Caleb stopped, an idea forming in his mind.

"What?"

"I could apply to be Dylan's foster parent."

The fury siphoning from her, Anne smiled. "That would be perfect! Then he wouldn't have to leave Chestnut Grove if there wasn't another family to take him in. He's been making friends here. I would hate to take that away from him. And the best part is, you can work with him and maybe help him."

Caleb started the engine. "It might work."

"It will work. I have a good feeling about it."

He slanted a look toward Anne. "It's dinnertime. Want to go grab something to eat at the Starlight Diner?"

"I—I—" Flustered, Anne snapped her mouth closed, color tingeing her cheeks a pretty rosy hue.

"What? No? Yes?"

She nodded.

"Good. I've just realized I'm starved. It's been a long day looking for a runaway, making flyers, dealing with Rex Givens. I hope you're hungry, because I'm planning on having dessert in celebration."

"Celebration?"

"Yeah. Hopefully I've found a way to help Dylan." Caleb's spirits lifted even more when he saw the smile grow on Anne's face. He grinned in return, feeling like a teenage boy discovering the appeal of girls.

"What if the Givens decide to keep Dylan?"

Pulling away from their house, Caleb said, "I've got the feeling they won't mind me applying for the job. They'll probably welcome it. From what Rex said, they would much rather have an easier child to parent."

"And if Dylan leaves their house, they'll have room for another one?"

"Yep."

Anne thought of her own parents and their

lack of involvement in raising her. They had been wrapped up in their teaching at the college and their research projects. Although she still lived with them, even now she rarely saw her parents. She sometimes wondered if the only reason they had wanted her to live with them—in fact, they'd insisted—was so she could watch the house when they were gone, which was a lot lately with her father on the lecture circuit.

"Parenting shouldn't be a business," Anne said, then instantly regretted revealing her thoughts. She bit down on the inside of her cheek to keep from expounding on the subject.

Caleb stopped at a red light, throwing her a glance. "I agree. Being a parent is the most important job there is, and it should never be taken lightly or for granted."

"Are your parents still alive?"

"No. They were in their forties when they had me. They tried for years and had actually given up when I came along. They told everyone I was God's little surprise for them." Pressing his foot on the accelerator, he drove through the intersection.

Anne heard the love in his voice. "Then you were an only child?"

"Yes. Even though my parents were older,

I kept bugging them for a brother. It never happened." He parked in front of the diner and switched off the engine, angling toward her. "I didn't like being an only child. When I have a family, I want a whole house full of children. How about you?"

"I was an only child, too. I didn't much like it, either." She purposely avoided answering him about having children of her own. She also wanted a whole house full of them, but she didn't think that would happen. Her marriage prospects were slim. They shared a dream but not a future.

He started to say something, seemed to think about it and decided not to. Instead, he turned away and got out of the car. Hurrying around the front of the car, he opened her door for her before she had a chance to gather her purse from the floor and do it herself. For a second she almost felt as if she was on a real date, but then reality hit when she glimpsed herself and Caleb in the plate glass window along the front of the diner. They were such an unlikely pair. The best she could hope for with Caleb Williams was friendship.

Inside he grabbed a booth with bright blue vinyl seats near the front and slid in, peering at the poster of James Dean on the wall above him. She gave James a quick smile. An old Elvis song played on the jukebox at the back of the diner, its catchy tune causing her to tap her foot to the beat. So many odors vied for dominance. Anne drew in a deep breath and relished the scent of beef sizzling above all the other aromas.

"Hmm." He flipped open the menu. "It always smells so good in here. I wish I was a better cook than I am."

"You don't cook?"

He shook his head. "What I do when I'm desperate isn't what you would really call cooking. I have a lot of frozen dinners and prepared foods. How about you? Do you like to cook?"

"I can cook, but I can't say that I like to. It's not that much fun to cook for just yourself."

"Don't you live with your parents?"

"Yes, but they aren't home that much to eat what I make, so I resort to frozen dinners, too." Anne opened the menu and skimmed it, already knowing what she was going to have.

When the waitress, Miranda Jones, came to the table a few minutes later, Caleb gave her their orders, then took a long sip of his ice water. "I'm so relieved that you'll be helping with the decorations this week. I hope it won't be too much extra work for you."

Unwrapping her utensils, Anne smoothed her napkin in her lap. "No. The only night I can't make it is Wednesday night. I volunteer to hold babies at the hospital that evening."

"Hold babies?"

"Actually, I usually do it twice a week, but I think I can get someone to do my Friday shift since that's when we'll be putting up all the decorations for the carnival on Saturday." She leaned forward, loving the topic of conversation. "I sit in a rocking chair and hold, talk to and even feed the babies, who need someone to do it for them. There are some babies—many of them preemies—who are in the hospital for weeks and need to be held and loved, either because their parents can't always be there to do it or because they don't have parents who want to. I think it's the best job in the world." *Especially since I don't know if I will ever have my own children to hold,* she silently added.

"I didn't realize there was such a job. You're right. It would be great. You would probably enjoy working in our nursery on Sunday."

Anne stared down at her plate. She knew so little about God and Jesus, only what

Grandma Rose had told her as a little girl. When her gaze returned to his, she said, "I can't remember the last time I've been to a church for a service other than a funeral or a wedding."

Chapter Three

Caleb relaxed back in his seat, the noise of the jukebox and the patrons in the diner fading into the background as he riveted his attention to Anne. "Then you should come to our service one Sunday."

"I don't know." She fidgeted with her napkin, balling it up. "My parents are atheists."

"And you?" Caleb gritted his teeth, almost afraid to hear her reply.

"Confused. I don't know what I am. When I was a little girl, I used to visit my grandma and go to church with her. Then I would come home and my parents would have nothing to do with going to church even when I would ask them about it."

The tension washed from him as he sat forward, placing his elbows on the table. "On

Sunday afternoons I have a group at the center. We discuss our faith, the Bible, the challenges of being a Christian in today's world. Come join us. Some talk, some just listen."

"I don't know. I—I'll think about it."

"We start at three and go till we finish."

"No set time to end?"

"Sometimes we're in a talkative mood, other times not. There's no pressure put on the group. It's a time to explore our faith."

Miranda brought their dinners and first placed Anne's plate in front of her, then Caleb's. The scent of roast beef, slathered in a thick, brown gravy, wafted to him, reminding him he was hungry. He watched Anne pick at her cheeseburger and fries and wondered what she was thinking.

Lord, help me to reach her. She needs me. She needs You in her life.

Caleb listened to Gina give the opening prayer before they began their Sunday afternoon faith session. When the girl finished, his gaze slid toward the door into the TV room at the center. Was Anne going to come? he wondered, fighting the disappointment that she wasn't sitting with them.

He could remember Teresa in college and their long talks about God. He'd thought he could show her the importance of the Lord, but in the end he hadn't been able to and he'd had to acknowledge he couldn't marry someone who didn't believe as he did. He would have been asking for trouble before their marriage even began. Cutting his losses had hurt him deeply because he had loved Teresa, but when he married, it would be for a lifetime.

"A friend at school asked me the other day that if Jesus was really the son of God, then why did He die like He did? Why didn't He just save himself?"

Jeremy's question pulled Caleb out of the past and firmly in the present. "What do you all think?" He scanned the fourteen faces of the teenagers in the group.

Tiffany waved her hand in the air, bouncing up and down on her chair. "I know why. I know! He died for our sins."

"He died because He was finished with His message to us. Christ had done what He was sent to do," Gina added.

As Billy gave his opinion, Caleb saw Anne at the doorway. She listened to the different children's opinions but didn't come any farther into the room. A lightness entered his heart at the thought she had come to hear about God. There was hope.

Leaning forward, Caleb rested his elbows

on his thighs, clasping his hands loosely together. "What you say is all true. But more importantly, Jesus was resurrected to show us the way, to show us not to fear death, that He would be waiting for us when our time came. No other has come back from the dead like He did." As Caleb talked, he noticed Anne step into the room. "He wanted His disciples to go out into the world and spread His word. And Christ wanted no doubt in their minds who He was. How would you have responded if He had shown Himself to you three days after He had died?"

Anne eased into a chair next to Nikki near the door. The young girl bent toward Anne and said something to her. Anne smiled, then glanced at him. Caleb's heartbeat increased. The sound of voices melted away while his attention clung to Anne across the room, experiencing a connection to her that he hadn't before.

She was here. She had taken her first step toward the Lord. His heart sang with the news and all the possibilities. Hope flared into a full-blown promise.

An hour later when the discussion died down, Gina announced, "I brought brownies for anyone who is hungry."

The teenagers made their way to the table along the west wall where the brownies and some soda were set up. Anne hung back, moving toward the door.

"You aren't going to leave without saying hi, are you?" Caleb asked, eager to see what her impression of the session was.

"Hi." She sidled a step closer to the door. "You didn't tell me I would be one of two adults at this meeting."

He shrugged. "I didn't think it was important. You know everyone here." He spread his arms wide. "What did you think?" He positioned himself between Anne and the door, not wanting her to leave just yet.

"Interesting. I particularly liked Billy's comment about seeing Jesus after He died."

"I think 'wow' just about sums it all up. Leave it to a child to put it into one word."

"Kids do have a way of getting to the point."

"So?" He propped his shoulder against the door frame, folding his arms over his chest, hoping he appeared casual, nonchalant.

"This past hour has given me a lot to think about." Anne looked back at the group. "Where's Dylan?"

"He's never come to one of these meetings."

"So you haven't had time to talk with him anymore?"

He shook his head. "But we're going to meet tomorrow after school."

"Before we work on the decorations?"

"Yep."

"Anne, it's nice to see you here," Gina said, interrupting them. "Want a brownie?" She held up a nearly empty plate, thrusting it between Anne and Caleb.

"I'd better not. If I ate one, I would want two."

"There's nothing wrong with having two brownies. How about you, Caleb?"

"Thanks." Caleb took one from the plate, his palms sweaty.

"Catch y'all later. Got to get rid of the rest of these. I can't take them home! Mom would *so* not be happy." She went back to the other kids for a soda.

"Only a child who is reed thin would say that about two brownies," Anne said with a laugh, looking up at Caleb.

"I'm glad you came."

She pinned him with an intense look. "Why?"

"Because I want you to experience Jesus as I do." Which was true, but Caleb wondered if it wasn't more than that.

Caleb read the e-mail from Kimberly Forrester a second time before deleting it. He missed the theology talks over coffee they'd had while they'd both been missionaries together at the same mission in Africa. He missed their friendship, which had grown while working together, and wished an ocean didn't separate them, but he understood her need to serve God the way she thought He wanted. In her e-mail it sounded as if she was accomplishing what she had set out to do. He was glad for her, but it left his own failure to reach Dylan as a disappointment.

Yesterday at their first formal counseling session, the boy hadn't said more than two words—good bye—at the end of the longest fifteen minutes Caleb had experienced. He would try again today and prayed he could get through to the boy.

Shutting down his computer, Caleb rose to see what was keeping Dylan. He should have been here by now. When he walked outside, he noticed the boy sitting on the steps, chin resting in his palms, shoulders hunched.

"Dylan, I was worried about you."

Dylan remained silent, his face averted.

Caleb eased down next to the boy who twisted away. "What's wrong?"

"If you must know," Dylan muttered and brought his face around for Caleb to see.

"How did you get that nasty cut?"

"A fight."

"When? With who?"

"Today after school." The boy squared his shoulders, defiance in his expression now, as though he silently challenged Caleb to say anything about him fighting.

"What happened?"

"I got tired of a couple of guys making fun of me. I decided to fight back." Dylan's eyes narrowed, his body stiff, as though he were ready to fight all over again.

"Did fighting solve your problem?"

The child shot to his feet, his hands fisted. "Yes. They'll think twice before taunting me again."

"What were they taunting you about?" Caleb rose slowly, weary from lack of sleep and concern over Dylan.

His knuckles whitened, his body grew even more rigid. "Because my father is a drunk. Because—" He whirled about and raced up the steps, disappearing into the center.

Caleb heaved a sigh and followed the boy into the building, the anger he felt gripping Dylan charging the air with an intensity that was thick, heavy. He found him in the TV room, watching a program. Caleb walked over and switched off the set. Dylan's mouth firmed into a scowl, his forehead creased with deep lines. He lowered his gaze, staring at the floor at his feet.

"We need to talk about this." Caleb moved toward the boy.

Dylan jerked his head up and stabbed him with an angry look. "No, we don't. I don't care what people think. I was just tired of them talking to me." He turned away as though Caleb wasn't in the room.

Rage encompassed every inch of Dylan. Caleb was at a loss about what to do to help him. *Please, Lord. I need Your guidance more than ever with this one. I can't fail him.*

"You know, Dylan, no matter what you do, I am still here for you. I care about you, enough that I have put in an application to be a foster parent. *Your* foster parent."

The only sign Dylan heard his words was a slight stiffening. Otherwise his head remained averted, his lower lip stuck out in a pout, his arms crossed over his chest. Silence eroded Caleb's confidence that one day he would be able to reach him. He moved to stand in the boy's direct line of vision.

"I didn't ask you to be my foster parent," Dylan finally muttered, his gaze lifting to Caleb's.

"I know. I want to be."

"Why?"

"Because I think we need each other."

"I don't need you." Dylan dropped his gaze away, hugging his arms to his chest.

"But I need you."

For a long moment Caleb wasn't even sure that Dylan had heard him this time. Then the boy drew in his lower lip and chewed on it, his shoulders now bowed as though he were an old man. In many ways he had seen more of the darker side of life than most at his age. Thinking about the boy's past only reaffirmed Caleb's need to pierce through Dylan's armor and reach him. He hadn't lied to the child. He needed him.

Dylan was his chance to right a wrong.

Tension knotted Anne's neck, causing her shoulders to ache and a dull pain to throb behind her eyes. She stood and stretched, rolling her head. She had spent an hour looking through the old ledgers, and yet, she hadn't found anything to help Kelly. Maybe the answers weren't in the books, but she couldn't rule them out.

Checking her watch, she hurriedly shut the book and put it on the top of the stack of old ledgers for the adoption agency. She hadn't realized how late it was. She needed to get to the youth center to help make the decorations for the carnival. With a glance out the window she noticed that dusk began to blanket the landscape.

Snatching up her purse, she rushed from her office, arriving at the center ten minutes later. The lights in the building blazed as the dark shadows of night crept closer. She was never late, but she had become so absorbed earlier in the ledgers that she'd lost track of time, which was most unusual for her. Lately she had felt many things about her life weren't usual. She didn't like not having control over what was going on. But worse, she was wrestling with whom she was, questioning how she saw herself.

In the arts-and-crafts room, Caleb looked up from sprinkling silver glitter all over a large star. "I was wondering where you were. I was going to give you fifteen more minutes and then send out a posse."

"Yeah. I've never seen someone look at the clock so much," Gina mumbled, whisking the star away from Caleb and replacing it with another one to be decorated. "He was cutting out the stars until he cut off one of the points. He's been banned from using a pair of scissors."

Anne offered a weak smile. "Sorry I'm

late. I got busy and forgot the time. What do you need me to do?"

"Help Caleb with the stars." Gina moved over to let Anne sit next to him. "He needs help. *Desperately*."

"Hey, I'm not that bad," Caleb muttered and proceeded to dump more glitter on the table than the star in front of him.

As Anne worked, her arm brushed against Caleb's. She started to scoot her chair over to give them more room but noticed that Gina had her penned in. The teenager flashed her a smile and winked. If Anne didn't know better, she would think that Gina was sitting too close on purpose. But why would she do that?

Caleb reached for another star and their arms touched again. "Sorry about that. It's a little crowded in here."

He turned to Nikki next to him and asked her to move over. Her chair scraped across the wooden floor maybe a whole two inches. Caleb gave her a quizzical look. The child busied herself with cutting out a star.

He bent close to Anne's ear and whispered, "Is something going on that you and I don't know about?"

She shrugged, unable to say anything because all her senses honed in on Caleb's nearness that brought his scent wafting to her nose. His warm breath fanned her skin below her ear until it became hot and cold at the same time.

"Guys, give us some room here," Caleb said after he nearly elbowed Anne in the side while reaching for another star. "Maybe one of you could work at the other table or I could—"

Nikki shot to her feet, toppling over her chair in her haste. "I'll move. You can stay put."

After the girl took her paper and scissors and parked herself at the other table with Billy, Dylan and Jeremy, Caleb righted Nikki's chair, then moved it around so he could scoot his down. Disappointment fluttered through Anne now that she had breathing room.

"I tried, Anne," Gina whispered.

Anne peered at the girl. "Tried what?"

Gina tossed her head in the direction of Caleb. "You know, to help you with Caleb."

"Help me?" Her question squeaked out louder than Anne had intended. A few people, including Caleb, glanced her way. She edged toward Gina and lowered her voice, asking, "What are you all up to?"

"Oh, nothing. Just helping a friend get

what she wants." Gina straightened away from her, winked again and resumed working.

Short of making a scene Anne didn't think she would get anything else out of Gina—like what in the world was she up to. But she knew now that the girl thought she had a crush on Caleb—which she did. Embarrassment burned her cheeks as she thought of who else might think that. She hoped Caleb was clueless. If she thought he realized how she felt, she would—she wasn't sure what she would do.

While reaching for the glitter, she chanced a look toward Caleb, and just at that moment, he lifted his head. He smiled at her. Warmth flushed her. When his gaze caught hers and held it, she didn't look at what she was doing. Her fingers fumbled. The jar tipped over, scattering silver glitter all over the table, completely outdoing Caleb's earlier sloppiness.

The sound of the plastic container rolling off the table and bouncing on the floor dominated the sudden silence. Caleb peered away, breaking his visual hold while she saw the mess she'd made and cringed. Leaping to her feet, she tried to clean up all the glitter. Caleb rose, too. Her hands shook as she swept the silver sprinkles into a pile while he scooped them up into the jar. She felt as though she were all thumbs, not able to do anything right when she was in his presence. She'd never had this problem before meeting Caleb Williams. What must he think of her?

"No harm done," Caleb said, setting the jar back on the table, minus just a little silver glitter.

"You know, Anne, that's not a bad idea for us to sprinkle glitter all around," Gina said. "It adds a special touch to the room."

"You didn't say that when I spilled some," Caleb interjected with humor in his voice.

"Yeah, I like it, Gina," Tiffany said while the guys groaned.

"There'll be enough swords and dragons for you all, so a little glitter won't hurt," Nikki said to the boys.

"A little!" Jeremy snorted. "I'll be tracking this all over the place. Mom won't let me in the house."

Anne noticed Dylan lower his head and appear as though what he was cutting out was the most fascinating activity he could do. He hung out on the fringe, much as she had done while growing up.

"A little glitter never hurt anyone. It makes the world sparkle." Nikki took the glitter she was working with and tossed some at Jeremy.

He jumped back, his chair crashing to the floor. He grabbed the jar that had begun this whole episode, cupped his hand and poured some into it. He started around the table to get at Nikki. She shrieked and ran to Caleb.

Laughing, he sidestepped at the exact second Jeremy threw the silver glitter at Nikki, who managed to leap away, too. The sparkles caught the light and gleamed as they floated to the floor.

"I guess that pretty well takes care of whether or not we're going to have glitter scattered about," Caleb murmured to Anne before moving forward and raising his hands. "Let's stop right there. We have too much to do to get into a glitter fight. We've only done half the stars so far."

The kids groaned and got back to work.

"Tsk. Tsk. What a taskmaster." Anne hoped that her expression was pure innocence and by the chuckle she received from Caleb it must have been.

"Do you want to volunteer to keep them in line?"

His question produced her own laugh. "No way. I know when I'm outmanned and outsmarted. No wonder you gave in to Gina about them running the carnival this year. Much easier in the long run."

"You aren't implying I let them get away with murder, are you?"

She splayed her hand over her heart. "Who me? At least you're willing to try. I can't imagine working with a whole center of youths, many of them with raging hormones."

Caleb gave her a pair of scissors and took the glitter from in front of her. "You cut. I'll glitter."

"You trust me with scissors but not the glitter?"

"Yep, you have to be a better cutter than I am. Remember the four-pointed star."

"I think Gina's idea of the stars hanging down from the ceiling will give it a festive air."

"That's the point or so she says."

Anne leaned closer to Caleb. "She's quite a young lady."

He glanced toward the teen. "Yeah, she's going to go far in life. Knows what she wants and goes after it."

"I wish I had been more like that in high school."

"How about now?"

Anne tilted her head and pressed her lips together. "You know I can't say I'm that, even now."

"What do you want that you don't have?"

A family. Lots of children. Someone to share my life with. Those wishes flittered through her thoughts, but she wasn't going to share them with him. She'd learned a long time ago to keep things to herself. Much safer and less painful in the long run. "I wish I was more assertive."

"If I could, I'd grant you your wish."

"But you can't so I'm on my own."

Caleb looked her in the eye. "You are never on your own or alone, Anne. God is always with you."

Anne concentrated on cutting out the star she held, willing her hands to keep from quavering. She could remember Grandma Rose telling her the same thing right before she came back to Chestnut Grove after visiting her for the summer. But she'd felt alone except when she'd been with her grandmother. Anne's teeth dug into her lower lip to keep the tears from spilling into her eyes. She still mourned the loss of Grandma Rose after twelve years. Her best times while growing up had been with her grandmother on the farm.

As the hour progressed, Gina drew the stars, Anne cut them out and Caleb decorated them while the other kids had an assembly line going, too. Anne enjoyed listening to different stories about their day at school or something they had done recently. Everyone shared an incident except Dylan. As she watched the eleven-year-old, the youngest in the group, her heart went out to him. She thought back to her days in school and knew what it was like to be an outsider looking in. There were times she still experienced the feeling, even though she had good friends in Meg, Pilar and Rachel, friends she could count on. Dylan obviously felt he was alone, with no one to count on but himself. She saw it in his eyes.

A pizza delivery man appeared in the doorway with four large boxes and several plastic bottles of pop. While Caleb paid him, Gina took the pizzas and put them on the tables. Tiffany went into the kitchen and retrieved some paper cups and plates.

"I didn't know we were going to have dinner tonight," Anne said to Gina as the teenager stacked the napkins next to the first box.

"If we stay a little longer this evening we should be through with making the decorations. All that will be left for Friday and Saturday is putting it together. Caleb said the pizzas were our incentive."

"And a good one at that." Anne grabbed a plate and put two slices, one with pepperoni and the other with Canadian bacon, on it. "I don't usually have pizza, but I love it."

"Why not?"

"Too many calories."

"But you're thin."

"That's *why* I'm thin. I watch what I eat. If I ate what I wanted, I would be a good twenty or thirty pounds heavier. It's a constant battle to keep the pounds off."

Gina stared at her a long moment and asked, "Why is it that people aren't satisfied with what God gave us? No one is perfect. We all have things wrong with us."

Anne glanced down at her feet, turned in slightly even after all this time wearing corrective shoes. She remembered the years of taunts she'd endured and shuddered. "That's a good question, Gina."

"You know God doesn't give us any more than we can handle."

"He doesn't?"

"I was angry at God when my father died last year, but Caleb helped me to see that the Lord is with me always. His love will get me through anything I have to deal with. I'll be reunited with my father one day. I'll always carry the memory of him around in my heart and what he taught me will be with me, too. Nothing can take that away."

Anne marveled at how mature Gina was. No wonder the carnival preparations were coming along fine. What if she had believed in the Lord while growing up? Would she had felt so alone with her troubles? Would she have been able to brave the taunts of others with God in her heart?

"What would you like to drink?" Caleb asked as he untwisted the cap on one of the soda bottles.

"That will be fine." Anne took a paper cup and held it up while Caleb poured some of the clear pop for her. Sitting down where she'd been working, she pushed the stars across the table so they were out of harm's way and dug into her pizza. "What time are we going to call it quits?"

His mouth full, Caleb finished chewing before answering, "Eight-thirty. It's a school night."

"Do you think we'll get it all done by then?"

Caleb scanned the unfinished stars, the last item to be done before Friday. "I think. If not, I'll be cutting and glittering through the wee hours."

"If you need any help, I can stay. It's not a school night for me."

"You say that like a person who is glad to be out of school."

"Not my best years."

"I have to admit it wouldn't be a time I would want to repeat. Too many ups and downs."

Anne couldn't look at Caleb. She was afraid all the pain she had experienced would be reflected in her expression. She wanted to keep her past in the past, not reexamine something she couldn't change.

Fifteen minutes later Anne started cutting out more stars. She was sure she would wake up in the middle of the night, moving her hands as though she were still cutting out stars. By the time eight-thirty arrived, everything was finished except five sheets of four stars. Some of the kids left with their parents , and Jeremy drove the rest home.

"You don't have to stay." Caleb sprinkled some glitter on a star.

"It'll go twice as fast if I stay. There's no one home waiting for me."

"I know you live with your parents. Where are they?"

"My dad's lecturing at a conference and Mom went with him. They're gone a lot. That's why I stay there, to take care of the house."

"I called Dylan's case manager today about applying to be his foster parent. I'm going to see Mrs. Davis tomorrow about it."

"That's wonderful. Did you notice that Dylan didn't say anything tonight?"

"You saw his face. Tomorrow he'll have a black eye."

"What happened?"

"A fight after school."

"There's a lot of anger in him."

Caleb sighed. "I know and he won't tell me about it."

"Give him time. Hopefully he will."

"But what if he does something stupid before I have a chance to reach him?"

The anguish in Caleb's voice riveted her attention to him. "Like what?"

He waved his hand in the air, all his frus tration evident in the gesture. "I don't know. Run away again, or something worse."

"You're thinking suicide?"

The anguish crept into his expression, taking over. "It is a possibility."

"Yes, I guess it is, but Dylan seems like a fighter to me."

"Because of the fight?"

"No, more than that. Right at the moment he's screaming out loud and clear he's in trouble. He may not be telling you what's wrong, but you know something is wrong. I think he'll break his silence in his own time."

"I pray to God he does. I don't want to think—" Caleb's voice faded into the silence.

Anne wanted to question him further, but his expression became closed, completely shutting her out. Something was bothering Caleb, and like Dylan hopefully he would share it with her in his own time. They wouldn't be anything more than friends, but at least Anne wanted that friendship with Caleb.

When he put the finishing touches on the last star, he announced, "Done. I don't want to see another star for a long time."

"Then I suggest when you leave here you don't look up at the sky." Anne nodded her head toward the window over Caleb's shoulder. "It looks like a clear fall evening outside."

He stood and began cleaning up. "I'll keep that in mind."

With Anne's help the room was back to normal in fifteen minutes with minimal glitter on the wooden floor and tables. She stood at the door with broom and dustpan in hand and surveyed the area. "So this will be transformed into a picture-taking room on Saturday?"

"The plans call for that."

"I still hear skepticism in your voice."

"I know Gina's a genius and so organized I'm amazed, but I don't think I'll breathe easy until Sunday when it's all over."

"The people who come would gladly give the money to the center for the rec equipment so don't fret too much."

"Aye, aye, ma'am." Caleb saluted her, then whisked the broom and dustpan from her hands. "I'll put them away. Will you make sure all the lights are off?"

As Anne made the rounds of the other rooms, she noticed the overhead lights were off in the TV room, but a soft glow illuminated the darkness. Someone must have left the TV on. She went inside to switch it off and saw Dylan watching a show. As she came around the tall sofa and got a good look at him in the light, tears streamed down his cheeks. He saw her. Quickly he clicked off the set while swiping at his face.

Even though it was dark, Anne felt her way to the couch. She didn't say anything but sat down next to the boy and waited.

Chapter Four

"Anne? Anne, where are you?"

She heard Caleb calling her and felt Dylan go rigid next to her on the couch in the TV room. She slipped her hand over his fist, which lay between them. He didn't pull away, but instead sniffed as though he was trying to get his emotions under control.

"Do you want me to give you a ride home, Dylan?"

For a long moment the boy said nothing.

"Anne," Caleb called from the hallway.

"I guess so," Dylan mumbled as Caleb flipped on the overhead light and illumination flooded the room.

Anne rose and faced Caleb. "Sorry, Dylan and I were talking. I'm gonna give him a ride home."

"I can. It's on my way." Caleb moved farther into the room.

His head hung down, Dylan slowly got to his feet. Silence lay heavy in the air for a long moment.

"That's okay. I can do it." Anne hated making an issue of this with Caleb, but she had told Dylan she would drive him home and she wouldn't break her word to him—not even over something as little as who took him home. She had a feeling a lot of people had let the boy down in the past. This small thing was important to their relationship. "Are you ready, Dylan? I don't know about you, but I'm tired after this long day."

Anne walked past Caleb, realizing she should explain about Dylan. She paused in the hallway, saying to the boy, "I'll be with you in a sec," then hurried back to Caleb. "There's something about Dylan's situation at school that was similar to mine. Let me see if I can reach him."

The puzzled look on Caleb's face vanished. "I hope you can. I'll be picking up the girls at the agency tomorrow. I'll stop by your office and talk to you. I need all the help you can give me to get through to Dylan."

His plea added to her growing list of reasons why she liked this man. He wasn't afraid to ask someone for help. She could learn from Caleb on that score. She gave him a smile, then rushed back to Dylan before he decided to leave on his own.

Out in her car she strapped on her seat belt, then waited for Dylan to do likewise. When he didn't, she said, "I don't drive without everyone in my car buckling up."

"Why?"

There was a world of defiance in the question. Why had she thought she could reach him? In fact, she had witnessed him crying, which might alienate him even more. Maybe Caleb should have driven the boy home. All her doubts washed over her in that moment.

Studying Dylan, who needed someone to care about him, she determinedly put her worries away. "Because I had a friend once whose life was saved because she was wearing one."

He buckled his belt, the click sounding loud in the sudden silence. Anne switched on the car and pulled out of the parking lot.

Five minutes away from the Givens' house she said, "You know, Dylan, I won't say anything about what happened back there unless you want me to."

Silence.

Anne searched her mind for a way to reach

him. "I don't talk about this much with others, but when I was in school, kids used to taunt me about the funny shoes I wore and the way I walked. It really bothered me a lot."

"I don't care what the others say."

Anger laced each word and tore at Anne's heart. In a split second she relived all the hurts she'd had while growing up, and the many times she denied to herself and others that she cared what some kids said. She'd had no one to turn to except Grandma Rose, who lived hundreds of miles away, and later, in middle and high school, Pilar, Rachel and Meg. But by the time she had formed her friendship with the three, the damage had been done. She wasn't going to let Dylan go through it alone. "What doesn't bother you?"

"That my father loves to drink more than he loves me."

A tightness about her chest gripped her, squeezing the air out of her lungs. "How did they know about your father?"

"Mandy said something to one of her friends. She used to be the oldest at the Givens'. Now I am. I don't think she likes that."

"Jealousy can make people do things that aren't nice."

"I don't care. My dad will get better and I'll leave soon."

Anne's hands clenched the steering wheel as she turned onto the Givens' street. The house loomed up ahead and there was so much she wanted to say to Dylan. And yet, she wasn't sure where to begin.

"Dylan, what if your father doesn't get better?"

"He will. He—"

Anne stopped the car in front of the house and looked over at Dylan. The streetlight afforded her a view of his face she wished she hadn't seen. Anguish marked his features as he fought to keep from crying again. But a lone tear streaked down his cheek, then another.

"You are not alone, Dylan."

"Yeah. Yeah, I know. God is with me. That's what everyone tells me. If that's so, then why—" The child gulped and clamped his mouth shut.

"Why what?"

"Nothing," he mumbled, fidgeting with the handle.

"What I was going to say is that I care about you and so does Caleb. We're here for you."

Dylan yanked the door open. "Yeah, sure.

Thanks for the ride." He raced up the sidewalk to the house.

Anne waited until he disappeared inside before she pulled away from the curb. Turmoil churned in her stomach. She knew that Caleb had so much more experience at counseling than she. She had no idea how much good she'd done, if any, this evening, but she had to try and reach Dylan.

Anne massaged her temples, but nothing relieved the pounding in her head. The only light in her office came from between the slits in her blinds and the glare from her computer. Nausea bubbled in her stomach, threatening to rise. Gritting her teeth together, she tried to finish the last entry.

"Anne?"

She looked up to find Caleb in her doorway with Midnight, the resident cat, weaving in and out of his leg before ambling away. The dimness threw his expression in the shadows. Shutting down her computer cast the room into further darkness, but it soothed some of the hammering against her skull.

"Are you okay?"

"No," she managed to answer, rubbing her forehead, her eyes. "I have a migraine."

"Is there anything I can do?"

She closed her eyes for a few seconds, fighting the bile clogging her throat. "I'm supposed to volunteer at the hospital this evening holding babies. Can you take my place? I don't think I can do it, and I don't have time to find someone to replace me. I'm due there in a little over an hour."

He came into her office and stopped before her desk, concern etched into his features. "I'll take the girls home, then go. Which hospital?"

"Children's Hospital in Richmond."

"I'd better get going then." He turned away, paused and glanced back at her. "Can I do anything else for you? Have you taken anything for your headache?"

"Yes. I'll be fine. Thanks for helping me out." She tried to smile but the effort was too much. "I owe you one."

"Let me give you a ride home, too."

"Thanks, but I'll be okay once I get home and lie down. My medicine just needs a chance to kick in."

Her head pulsated with the pain, but Anne focused on doing one thing at a time. Rising slowly, she watched as Caleb left her office to retrieve Tiffany, Nikki and Gina from the conference room. She was thankful it wasn't too far to her house or she would have taken him up on the ride. She would make it before her migraine got too bad.

Out in the hall she saw the girls coming out of the conference room at the back, with Caleb right behind them. Their chattering stopped when they spied her. Gina hurried to her.

"You don't look well, Anne."

Caleb frowned and approached, too. "I'm giving you a ride home. No arguments. You're white as a sheet and your hands are trembling."

Anne clutched her purse tighter in an effort to control the quivering. She didn't have the strength to fight Caleb and the girls. Besides, she realized it wasn't wise to drive herself. "Fine."

He placed an arm about her shoulders and followed the three teenagers out to his Suburban. After assisting Anne into the front, he hurried to his side and climbed in. He twisted around and brought his finger to his lips to indicate the girls keep quiet. Worry gnawed at him as he threw the car into Drive and headed for Anne's. Her face was ashen and she huddled against the door as though she would like to curl into a ball to warm herself. He hated the helplessness that attacked him. He wanted to do more for Anne than take her place at the hospital.

When he pulled into the driveway at Anne's home, a weathered Colonial set back on a slightly overgrown piece of property, he realized this was the first time he had been to her house. "Are your parents home?"

"No, still gone." She pushed on the door to open it.

Caleb quickly slid from behind the wheel and rushed to help her to her front porch. "I don't like leaving you like this."

"Please. The babies are so important. They need to be held. Besides, the best thing for me right now is to lie down in a dark room until the worst has passed. My medicine is starting to work so there's nothing for you to worry about."

Looking at her still-pale features, he wasn't sure if there wasn't anything he needed to worry about, but he saw the determination in her expression and knew she wouldn't let him stay to take care of her. He took the key from her and inserted it into the lock. Even after she entered and shut the door, he didn't want to leave her. He stood on the porch for a moment before realizing he'd better get a move on or he would be late to the hospital. He didn't want Anne to have to be concerned about the babies. That was the least he could do. But he would be back.

* * *

Caleb cradled the small baby against his chest and rocked. He didn't want to leave, but he had already stayed an hour longer than he was scheduled to. The nurse came to take the child.

"It looks like the babies have recruited another volunteer," the young woman said.

"I was a goner when I picked up the first one."

"Most people are. I'm glad to see that you've signed up to help next Wednesday."

"I thought I would come with Anne."

The nurse put the baby back in his crib. "She's such a wonderful person. God doesn't make too many like her."

Caleb felt as if he had received the compliment just knowing Anne and being her friend. He thanked the woman and made his way to his Suburban. On the drive back to Chestnut Grove, he thought about Anne. Holding the babies tonight confirmed his desire to have a family even more. Anne would be a great mother. *God, why can't she believe in You?* If that were the case, he wouldn't have second thoughts about dating Anne and pursuing a relationship with her.

When he reached Chestnut Grove, he didn't drive to his apartment. Instead, he headed to Anne's, not sure what he would do when he arrived, but he had to make sure she was all right. He'd hated leaving her alone earlier, but it had been obvious she had known what to do with her migraine.

When he drove up to her house, he noticed a light on in the front room. That was all he needed to decide to check on her personally. Just in case she was in a sound sleep, he knocked on her front door rather than ringing her bell.

He started to leave when Anne opened the door, the light from the entry hall silhouetting her. "Hi. How are you feeling?"

Still dressed in her long black skirt and white blouse, she clasped the door frame, leaning into it. "Better. I wasn't sure if I was hearing things or if someone was really knocking at my door."

There were a few seconds of awkward silence, then Anne stepped back, swinging the door wider. "Since you're here, come inside and tell me how everything went tonight."

"Are you sure you're up to it?" he asked, walking into the house.

Her smile tilted up one corner of her mouth. "My head is only throbbing a little now and my stomach has settled down."

"But your head still hurts?"

She nodded, then winced.

"Maybe I should go."

She grabbed him to stop him from turning back toward the door. She glanced down at their clasped hands, her eyes widening. She released her hold and hurriedly said, "No, I want to hear about your experience. I hated missing my time with the babies."

Anne showed him into the front room, where a grouping of two tan chairs and one deep maroon couch sat in front of a set of floor-to-ceiling windows. A massive walnut desk and a series of bookcases, lined with countless books, were at the other end of the parlor. She motioned for him to have a seat in one of the chairs while she sat on the couch across from him.

"So what did you think?" Anne asked, dimming the light on the end table near her so it didn't glare in her eyes.

"That has got to be one of the best jobs in the world. Billy's 'wow' is an appropriate description of what I'm feeling."

The dullness of her eyes brightened. "That's the way I feel every time I go, especially for the babies who have no one to care for them."

"I enjoyed it so much I'm going back next Wednesday with you."

"You are?"

He grinned. "I thought we could go together and save on gas. What do you say?"

"I'm all for saving money." The brightness in her eyes spread to her facial expression, two dimples appearing in her cheeks.

"Good. I'm glad you and I can agree it would be beneficial for us to drive together to the hospital."

"Did you get anything for dinner?"

"I forgot all about dinner once I got there. I stayed an extra hour." However, the emptiness in the pit of his stomach couldn't be ignored for long. "I guess I'd better leave and grab something to eat on the way home."

Anne held up her hand, stopping him from rising. "Please, let me fix you a sandwich. That's the least I can do to thank you for filling in for me."

"I don't want you to go to any trouble." There was still a pallor to her skin, he thought, and wished he could take her pain completely away.

"It's no trouble. The worst is over." She started for the kitchen. "About all I can offer you, however, on such short notice is a sandwich. Is that okay?"

He quickened his step to catch up with her.

"Any food is okay with me. Remember, I don't cook so I really can't be too choosy."

"Oh, good. I have some leftover liver that should make a great sandwich."

Caleb cringed and gulped. "Well, maybe liver is the exception."

She smiled. "I was just kidding. I don't cook a lot, but believe me, liver will never be one of the things I cook." Anne opened the refrigerator and took all the makings of a turkey sandwich out and placed them on the counter near the sink.

"Are you going to have one?"

"Nope. My stomach is still a little queasy. If I get hungry, I'll make one later."

"Do you have migraines often?"

"Only when I get stressed and try to do too much." She dipped a butter knife into the mayonnaise, then spread it on the pieces of bread.

"Stressed? What about?"

"Let me see. Dylan, for one. Then there's the carnival and the mess with Tiny Blessings."

"I shouldn't have asked you to help with the carnival. I'm sorry. I didn't mean to add to your problems. I should be the only one worrying about it."

She swung around. "No, I'm glad you

asked. It isn't the carnival so much as Dylan and the problems with the adoption agency."

"What has Dylan said to you?"

Turning back toward the counter, Anne finished making his turkey sandwich and poured him a tall glass of milk. When she brought the dinner to the table where Caleb sat, she took the chair across from him.

"Dylan's having trouble at school with a few of the kids. They're making fun of him because his father is an alcoholic."

"Hence the fight?"

"Yes. But I think it's more than that. At the center, I see that he has made a few friends so he isn't alone at school. I think his main problem is the reason the state took him away from his father in the first place. Do you know the circumstances of his removal?"

"His father would leave him alone for days to fend for himself. The last time he was gone for five days and the school in Richmond notified the state."

"Any other abuse?"

"I suspect there was, but Dylan isn't saying." A memory from his own childhood crept into his thoughts. Another child who had kept silent, another child who had needed him. This time, he would be there to help.

"Then you need to get him to talk to you.

Something's eating at him that goes beyond being one of five children in the Givens' house or the kids at school taunting him."

Caleb lifted the sandwich, layered with lettuce, tomato and turkey and took a bite. After washing it down with a big gulp of milk, he said, "I'll try my best. Actually you might have better success than me. He seems to respond to you."

Anne looked away, her gaze trained on a spot behind Caleb. She'd had two parents who had provided a home for her. Even if they hadn't given her much emotional support, they had never abused her, just ignored her. "As a child I was never left to fend for myself, but I do know something of being taunted by the other kids at school."

"Why?" he asked, the beating of his heart slowing to a throb.

She gestured toward her feet. "Because I'm pigeon-toed. Because I looked a little different. Because I was painfully shy." She shrugged, trying to appear as if it hadn't mattered. "Who really knows why some students pick on others? Thankfully I found Meg, Pilar and Rachel. They helped me through some very dark times."

He reached across the table and covered

her hand with his. "From what I see and hear, you four are still good friends."

"We're there if anyone needs support. I couldn't ask for better friends than them." She slipped her hand free and laid it in her lap.

He missed the contact with her. He liked comforting her. "So how do you feel about your friends' recent marriages?"

A smile shone in her eyes. "Couldn't happen to better people! Eli, Jared and Zach are lucky men to have them as their wives."

"But that leaves you odd woman out?"

Her smile deepened. "I'll always be a part of their lives. But I won't kid you. I would like to get married one day. I want to have lots of children."

"So do I. Holding those babies tonight made the yearning stronger than ever."

"I know what you mean. I won't stop going to the hospital, but when I leave there, I can't help feeling just a little sad that one of those babies isn't mine." Anne pushed herself to her feet and went to the cabinet to retrieve a glass. She poured herself some ice water and drank several swallows before turning back to Caleb.

He finished his sandwich and wiped his mouth on the navy blue linen napkin Anne had set next to him. "I'd better be going. There are some last-minute things I need to do about the carnival. Will I see you Friday night?"

Anne straightened and put her glass down on the tan ceramic tile. "Of course. But I have to warn you, I'm not very handy with tools."

He bent toward her to say something and regretted the impulse immediately when her fresh apple scent teased his senses. He pulled back. "I won't tell if you won't tell I'm not very good, either."

"Then who is good that will be there?"

"Eli Cavanaugh's brother, Ben. He's a carpenter. He'd better be good with tools."

Chuckling, Anne made her way toward the front door. "True. If he isn't, then you are in big trouble."

"Now all I have to do is make sure he's going to be there Friday night."

"Is that one of your details you need to do tomorrow?" Anne opened the door for him.

He walked past her, then turned back toward her. "Afraid so. He wasn't sure and was going to let me know tomorrow."

"Do you have a back-up plan?"

"You're looking at the back-up plan."

Her chuckles evolved into robust laughter. "You'd better send up a prayer tonight."

"That's a given. Good night, Anne."

As he descended the steps outside, he heard the front door close behind him. This evening he had gotten a glimpse of the hurt that Anne had endured growing up. It was that hurt that had allowed her to connect with Dylan. He wished he had the power to erase their pain, but only God could do that. Sadness enveloped Caleb as he thought of what Anne was missing—the Lord's healing power.

Anne handed a silver glittered star to Caleb, who stood on the ladder waiting for it. "That will be the last one in here."

When Caleb finished attaching the clear plastic thread with the star at its end to the ceiling, he descended to the floor and stepped back, surveying his work. "It really does look wonderful."

Anne came to stand beside him. "Did you have your doubts?"

"Well—yes. I'm one of those people who doesn't fully get it until he sees it in front of his very eyes."

"Isn't there a story about a Doubting Thomas in your Bible?"

"Yes, there is. He wouldn't believe Jesus came back from the dead until he saw it with his own eyes."

"And?"

"Jesus appeared before him and showed him His scars from the nails."

"If it were only that easy to wipe away doubts."

"With God it can be that easy."

Was that all she needed to believe in herself? To believe in the Lord, in his unconditional love? She drew in a fortifying breath, expanding her lungs, then slowly released it through pursed lips. If only…

"What do we need to do next to this room?"

Caleb's question cut into her thoughts. "Set up the area where the photos are going to be taken."

"Has Ben finished making the castle backdrop?"

Anne listened for a few seconds. "It's awfully quiet out in the hall. I don't hear any more hammering, so I'm guessing he has."

"I'll help Ben move it in here if you'll go check on the others and please grab me a soda. All this work has made me thirsty."

This was the fourth time in the past hour of decorating the arts-and-crafts room that Caleb had come up with a reason to check on the others. He had allowed the kids to be in charge but wasn't quite able to let things go completely. She and Caleb had been given the task of transforming this room into a place for a photo opportunity. With the stars up and dangling from the ceiling, it was starting to come together.

"I know the castle backdrop is last-minute, but I'm sure glad that Ben and Jonah can do it. Ben does such good work. We'll get it painted and decorated in no time."

Caleb stopped her movement toward the door and placed his large hand on her forehead, a glint in his eyes. "Are you ill?"

She laughed. "No, and we will do it. We've got some time tonight and a good part of tomorrow."

"The carnival starts in—" Caleb peered at his watch "—in twenty-one hours!"

Her laughter increased. "I'm glad I'm here to be a calming effect on you." She was trying her best not to focus on the fact the man had his fingers around her arm, branding their imprint into her skin. "When Ben proposed building the scenery to go along with the fairy-tale theme, I thought it was a great idea."

"Yes, but we only have twenty-one hours and I don't know about you, but I need at least a few hours sleep."

"Now I see why Gina put you in here by yourself."

His gaze locked with hers. "I'm not by myself. You're here as the calming effect." His face split in a self-mocking grin that curled Anne's toes.

"And not doing a very good job."

He glanced down at his hand, his eyes widening as if he finally realized he was holding her, and released his grasp. He started toward the door. "Did I ever tell you about my time in college? Whenever a big assignment—or even a small one—was given out by the professor, I had it done right away. I never liked waiting until the last minute. People who did wait used to drive me crazy, rushing around, trying to get everything done." He opened the door and held it for her.

She walked past him into the hallway. "I have to admit I'm that way to a certain extent." Peeking over her shoulder at him, she continued, "But I am also flexible. I've learned to go with the flow most of the time."

"I'm working on it. God and I have had many talks about this very issue."

Caleb's references to the Lord made it seem as though God was his personal friend he chatted with every day. How could that be? "Did I not tell you Ben had it done?" She pointed toward the wooden structure taking up a good part of the hallway. "That's most of the job."

Caleb greeted Ben and his assistant, Jonah Fraser. Caleb tousled Ben's daughter's light brown hair. "Have you been helping your dad?"

Olivia nodded. "I've been handing him the nails."

"This was a family affair," Ben said while putting some of his tools into a box in a neat, organized arrangement.

"All I ask is next time get this brainstorm a little earlier than two days before the big event," Caleb said.

Ben held up his hands. "Not my fault. Gina didn't say anything until yesterday when she was baby-sitting Olivia."

"I've come to offer my services in moving this into the room." Caleb looked at Anne. "Don't you have something you need to do?"

"Men!" Anne shook her head, chuckling as she walked toward the largest room in the center that served as a cafeteria and gym for the youths.

Inside the room she immediately found Gina standing with Anne's friends, Meg and Rachel. The fifteen-year-old grinned when she saw Anne coming toward her.

"You're in here again?"

"Yes. Afraid so. This time I'm getting

Caleb a soda while he helps Ben and Jonah carry the castle backdrop into the room."

"They're done with it?" Gina asked.

"Yes. Where's the paint for it?"

"I brought some, my donation to the cause," Rachel said, gesturing toward an area by the door where several cans were stacked.

Meg scanned the room with groups of kids and adults helping to set up the booths for the carnival. "Do you want any help?"

Anne took a good look at Meg's attire and frowned. "In that outfit? I don't think so. You don't paint in nice slacks and silk blouses. What did you think you would be doing here this evening?"

Meg grimaced. "Nothing. I just stopped by to see what time I was needed tomorrow morning. I was working late at the office and haven't been home yet."

Anne put an arm around Meg. "Then go home. Your new husband might be a tad bit worried about you."

"Jared? It'll do him good to baby-sit for a while."

"Spoken like a mother of twins," Rachel interjected, smoothing back her long wavy chestnut hair, worn in a looser bun than usual.

"Okay, I'm going to rescue Jared, even

though he doesn't need it. He's great with Luke and Chance."

"Spoken like a woman in love," Anne said, heading for the kitchen to grab two sodas.

When she reappeared in the arts-and-crafts room a few minutes later, she found the three men grappling with the last large piece of scenery. When they finished putting together the backdrop—a castle with a turret and a drawbridge—Anne was impressed by how quickly Ben and Jonah had built it. Now all she and Caleb had to do was paint it to look like a castle. Thankfully it wasn't too large, just big enough for a group of people to stand on the "drawbridge" to have their picture taken for ten dollars.

"I've done my part. Now it's up to you two to make it look like a castle," Ben said, taking his daughter's hand and heading for the door.

When the trio left Caleb and Anne alone in the room, she studied the plywood structure, then swung her attention to Caleb. "We need help!"

"You think?"

Chapter Five

Anne caught sight of the clock in the gym and exhaled deeply, muttering to herself, "Three more hours and the big event will start." Thankfully, she'd gone home and caught a few hours' sleep.

"Do I hear panic in your voice?" Caleb whispered close to her ear, having come up behind her.

She jumped, startled by his appearance. Whirling about to face him, she said, "No, just stating a fact."

The corner of his mouth tilted upward and a gleam flashed in his eyes. "At least the paint on the castle is finally dry."

"How does it look?"

"Sparkly."

"That's what glitter does when applied to paint."

"But haven't you heard? Castles don't have glitter on them."

"Neither do stars. It adds a fairy-tale air."

"So you, Pilar and Rachel have told me."

"There, three to one. You lose."

He threw back his head and laughed. "Yes, I lose."

"You don't sound very concerned."

"I don't mind losing to three beautiful ladies."

Anne had to admit that both Pilar and Rachel were beautiful, but she was hardly in the same category. She bit her tongue rather than say anything to Caleb. She'd already revealed to him more about herself than she usually did with others. She was having too good a time to spoil the mood with her observations on how she looked. So she wasn't beautiful. She had other qualities—honesty, loyalty. If she kept listing them she would sound like a Boy—no, make that Girl—Scout.

"So now all we have to do is add the finishing touches to the castle and we're done." Anne started for the arts-and-crafts room.

"With that room," Caleb added, walking beside her. "But there's still a couple of booths that need setting up and—"

At the doorway into the gym, Anne came to a halt and lifted her hand close to his mouth to still his words. She didn't dare touch him or she might melt from the feel of his lips against her skin. "As you can see, Pilar and Gina are working on one booth and Jeremy and Meg on the other one. Everything has been taken care of. As soon as we complete the castle, we need to get our costumes on."

"What are you wearing?"

She turned into the hallway, shrugging. "Don't know. How about you?"

"Don't know, either. Gina is being particularly closed mouth about it. That's got me worried."

"She's probably done that on purpose. It gives you something other than the decorations for the carnival to worry about."

"I am not a worrier."

With one brow arched, Anne planted her hands on her waist and blocked his entrance into the room. "Say that again?"

"I do not worry excessively."

"Define 'excessive.'"

"Too much. More than is needed."

She directed her full attention to him. "You *do* worry too much and more than is needed." It was a quality that endeared him to her. She dropped her arms to her sides and entered the room. "There, I've done my calming job."

Caleb's laughter echoed through the multitude of stars hanging down from the ceiling. "I'm a job now?"

"Yes, and one of the more difficult ones Gina has assigned to me."

"I'm definitely having a word with that girl. She is way too smart for her own good."

Anne picked up a brush and a small can of green paint. "I hope you're good at making leaves."

"Better than cutting out stars."

"Well, then I am reassured."

Caleb snatched up his own brush and can. "I aim to please."

Anne chuckled, realizing these past few days getting ready for the carnival she had done a lot of that, mostly because of the man beside her. He attempted to paint ivy on the castle wall to soften the gray stone. He wasn't any Rembrandt but if you were nearsighted and standing across the room, what he was painting would vaguely look like ivy climbing up the castle wall.

An hour later, finished with the ivy and the other touches to make the stone facade look romantic, Anne stood back and examined their work. "Not too bad on such short notice."

"Ah-ha! You finally admit this was short notice."

"I never said it wasn't. But this castle was a much better idea than a trestle with artificial vines. This goes along with the theme for the evening, a fairy-tale wonderland."

Caleb pointed to the black area on the backdrop where the entrance into the castle would be if it were real. "Any moment I expect a knight to come charging out of there on a steed."

"Maybe you'll be a knight."

"I don't know if Gina is too happy with me right now. I wouldn't be too surprised if she gives me an ogre costume."

"To go along with your overbearing, grumpy disposition."

"I wasn't over—" he paused, his mouth curving down in a frown. "Okay, I was overbearing but not grumpy."

"There you two are." Gina came into the room, her hair a mess, and paint on her jeans and T-shirt.

"Where else would we be? You waved us toward this room yesterday and told us to do our best with it and not to come out until we did." Caleb spread his arms out wide. "So what do you think?"

Gina peered at Anne with sympathy in

her eyes. "Is this what you had to put up with all day?"

"Afraid so."

"I'm sorry."

"Hey, you two! I'm standing right here."

"It looks great. Ben did an excellent job on the castle."

"All he did was build it." Caleb pounded his chest. "*We* had to paint it."

"And you did an excellent job of painting it." Gina barely kept a straight face.

Caleb cupped one hand around his mouth and leaned toward Anne. "Do you get the impression we're underappreciated here?"

After walking toward the castle made of plywood and inspecting it, Gina whirled toward them and said, "And to show my *appreciation*, you both need to go home and get ready for the carnival."

"Okay, but what's happened in the other room?" Caleb peered toward the door. "I get the feeling you're trying to get rid of us."

"Boy, I'm gonna need a medal after this carnival for having to deal with him." Gina cocked her thumb toward Caleb. With a long sigh, she continued, "Everything's done in the other rooms. It's time we went home and cleaned up before we need to be back here. We only have two hours."

"That's plenty of time to throw on a costume."

Gina shook her head. "Anne, men just don't get it, do they?" She turned fully toward Caleb to explain, "Women don't throw on costumes or any other type of clothing. We have makeup to put on, hair to do—"

"I get the picture," Caleb interrupted, laughing. "I'm out of here. When do I get my costume?"

"Jeremy will bring it by your apartment in a while."

Caleb stopped walking toward the door and spun around, skepticism in his expression. "Why can't I get it before I leave?"

"Because Nikki's aunt isn't here yet."

"She isn't? I thought you said everything was taken care of."

Gina threw a beseeching look at Anne. "Help me."

"I think you're doing a great job all by yourself."

"Nikki's aunt is running a few minutes late but is already on the road with the costumes. She will be here soon. She called on her cell phone and told us. Go home. We have everything under control. Nikki, Jeremy and I are waiting for Nikki's aunt, then we're going home to get ready ourselves."

When Caleb left, mumbling something about taking an antacid, Gina shook her head slowly again, combing her fingers through her messy hair. "Remind me to let him do the whole thing next year all by himself."

"He worries."

"Whatever makes you say that?" Gina asked with a hint of sarcasm.

Needing to come to Caleb's defense, Anne said, "He wants this carnival to be a success because the equipment you have is falling apart. And the outreach program for after school with the low-income housing project is important to him."

"I know. It's important to us, too."

"Is my costume coming with Nikki's aunt?"

"Yup. We'll bring it to your house. Go home and relax in a nice bubble bath. There'll be a lot happening tonight."

"I think I will." Exhausted, Anne fought a yawn. The last thing she needed to do was sleep. She was afraid she wouldn't wake up until Sunday morning. "I haven't taken a bubble bath in ages. Sounds kinda nice."

"I'll see you soon."

After spending twenty minutes in a hot bubble bath that had left her fingers wrinkled, Anne felt almost human again. She tied the sash to her long white terry cloth robe tightly about her waist, then headed toward the kitchen to get some hot tea before she dressed for the evening.

After fixing a cup of raspberry tea, she sat at the kitchen table and sipped it. Should she call the center and see what was taking Nikki and Gina so long? Maybe Caleb was right to be worried. But if she didn't have a costume to wear, that would be all right with her. She'd help out at the carnival behind the scenes, where she liked to be.

The doorbell chimed. Anne took the last sip of tea, put the cup in the sink and hurried toward the door.

Gina, Nikki and Tiffany stood on her porch with huge smiles on their faces. Gina held a big white box while Tiffany carried a makeup bag. Warily, Anne opened the door wide for the girls to come inside.

"Thanks for bringing it by. What's my costume?" Anne started to reach for the white box, but Gina turned away and walked toward the stairs.

"Is your bedroom upstairs?"

"Yes," Anne answered slowly, her gaze glued to the rather large makeup bag that Tiffany held. "Why do you want to know?"

"We thought we would repay you for all your hard work this past week by helping you get ready." Nikki followed Gina up the stairs with Tiffany taking up the rear.

That left Anne at the bottom of the steps watching the trio disappear from view. The sound of the girls' footsteps above her jostled her out of her stunned state. Anne rushed upstairs, realizing she was going to regret offering her assistance if the impish looks on the girls' faces meant anything.

All three of them prowled the hallway outside her room, waiting impatiently for her. The door stood open.

"I like your room, Anne," Tiffany said when she saw her.

"You've kept all your old dolls and stuffed animals." Gina pointed toward the window seat where the childhood memories were. "Mom wants me to put mine in the attic. I can't. My dad gave me some of them." Then sensing this wasn't the time nor place to go into the topic, she started into Anne's room. "We'd better get to work if we're going to make the carnival on time. It's getting late."

Tiffany and Nikki disappeared into her room, too. Anne gripped the railing on the stairs, inhaled a calming breath and made her way to her doorway.

"You can leave the box on the bed. I appreciate your kind offer to help, but—"

Tiffany took her hand and led her over to her dresser. "Have a seat so we can get started."

"But—"

"Anne, let us do this for you." Gina placed her hands on Anne's shoulders and looked at her in the mirror. "Where should we start, girls?"

"Makeup. That's my specialty."

In her mirror Anne saw her eyes grow round at Nikki's comment. Nikki wore black lipstick and heavy black eyeliner against a pale complexion. And she considered herself an expert!

The fourteen-year-old laughed when she glimpsed Anne's expression. "I promise I'll use other colors besides black on you."

"I don't wear makeup. Besides, it's getting late and we wouldn't want to worry Caleb unnecessarily."

"This is a special night. Trust us, Anne. The reverend will be fine."

Gina's earnest appeal kept Anne from denying her wish. "Okay."

"Good. Tiffany, the bag please." Nikki waved the younger girl to her.

Nikki opened the bag and withdrew eye

shadow, foundation, powder, lipstick, eyeliner and blush. Then the girl took hold of Anne and whirled her around. "No peeking until I'm done."

Anne watched the minute hand on the clock sitting on her bedside table move excruciatingly slowly. She tried not to count the seconds and instead focused on the toile of her wallpaper with tiny pink rose bushes. The flowers began to blend into a massive bouquet. She glanced at the clock again and groaned. Five minutes had passed, and Nikki had only put on the foundation and powder.

Fifteen minutes and much consultation among the girls later, Nikki stepped back and swept her arm toward the mirror. "Have a look. What do you think?"

Slowly Anne inched around on the cushioned seat before her dresser. When she glimpsed her image in the mirror, she gasped, her hand covering her pink lips. A stranger stared back at her—a stranger with big, blue eyes highlighted with glittery silver eye shadow and midnight blue mascara and eyeliner. Her high cheekbones were dusted with a rosy shade much like the pink flowers of her wallpaper.

"I don't know what to say."

"How about you like it?" Nikki began to look doubtful.

Anne hurried to reassure her. "I like it. I'm not sure it's me, though."

"It's the new you—at least for tonight." Gina moved into Nikki's place behind her and whisked away the clip holding up Anne's ponytail.

Blond hair tumbled about Anne's shoulders. The teen ran a brush through it, her mouth pinched into a frown. Her eyes brightening, Gina held out her hand to Tiffany. "Scissors."

When the younger girl gave Gina the sharp apparatus, Anne came up off the seat. "I don't think—"

The instigator of this whole extreme makeover put her hands on Anne's shoulders and gently pushed her down. "Relax. My aunt fixes hair for a living. I've spent many days with her learning the finer points of doing hair. Do you think I would do anything to hurt you?"

Staring at the gleaming silver of the scissors in the teenager's hand, Anne wanted to shout yes, but she couldn't. Because in a strange way she did trust Gina. Her throat tight, Anne nodded her consent, then she immediately squeezed her eyes closed. The sound of the shears as they snipped away at her hair sent goosebumps skittering over her skin. Chilled, she tried to think of something nice and the only thing that popped into her mind was that she would be seeing Caleb that evening.

"You can open your eyes now," Gina said after dousing her with what sounded like a whole can of hairspray, the aroma overpowering. "Just want to make sure your hair stays in place."

Anne pried one eye open, the tightness in her throat expanding to her chest, making each breath she dragged in difficult. She was sure she was looking at someone else. It couldn't possibly be her in the mirror. Her hair fell to just below her chin, curling softly under and framing her face in a halo of gold. She now had bangs that feathered to one side, as well as a more layered look.

"You have beautiful hair." Gina came around to stand in front of Anne. "Do you like it?"

Stunned and speechless, Anne could only nod. Then she pinched herself to make sure she wasn't dreaming. Ouch! No, she was very much awake and a stranger in her own body.

Tiffany went to the bed and opened the

box. "We saved the best for last—your costume. Nikki's aunt brought this especially for you."

Anne scooted around on the seat before her dresser and watched as Tiffany unveiled her costume. The youngest girl lifted it out of the huge box. *Oh, my!*

Caleb tugged at the *thing* around his neck that was threatening to cut off his air supply. He tugged at the black satin sleeves of his coat, and the silver brocade of his vest, then glanced down at the silver stockings he wore under his knee-length pants and thought about hiding in his office until the carnival was over, except they were using his office as a costume store. So many people would be coming and going.

Where was his ogre outfit?

Jeremy surely had made a mistake and brought him the wrong box. Caleb looked at himself in the mirror over his dresser. Prince Charming! What had the kids been thinking when they picked this out for him?

Padding over to his chair, he sat and slipped on the black shoes—with a heel!—and a big silver buckle. When he stood, he wobbled and wondered if he would break his neck trying to walk in these shoes. He took a few shaky steps toward the door of his bedroom.

He could see the headlines now— "Youth minister dies trying to navigate in heels." Okay, so they weren't exactly heels, but they felt awkward to walk in. How did women do this on a regular basis?

Spying the clock on his beside table, he knew he better hurry if he was going to get there before the carnival started. He still wanted to check everything to make sure they were ready. Of course, he didn't know what he could do about it with only fifteen minutes to go.

Feeling totally silly driving a modern vehicle dressed in clothes from the eighteenth century, Caleb hoped no one saw him. But that wasn't to be. His neighbor across the street waved as he climbed into his white Suburban, and when he arrived at the center, there were already a couple of people waiting for the carnival to begin. He greeted them and rushed inside, his cheeks hot. His office was looking better and better as a place to hide even if it was where the extra costumes were stored.

Maybe he could change into something else. With that idea in mind, he started for his office when he saw through the doorway into the gym a vision in white and silver dash by. Who was that? Was there a problem?

He decided to check before he changed costumes. He made his way to the gym and peered inside. The vision in a white and silver gown stood by one of the food booths, leaning over the table, trying to reach something on a chair on the other side. He hurried over to help her.

She straightened with a rabbit in her hand. He slowed. She turned toward him and his heart slammed against his rib cage.

Anne!

Breathtaking in white satin with silver accents that were even in her golden hair, as though she were a fairy-tale princess.

Hugging the rabbit to her, she saw him and her eyes grew round. "They got you, too."

He bowed from the waist. "Prince Charming, at your service."

She swept one arm across her body. "I think I'm supposed to be Cinderella."

"Does that mean you have to leave at midnight?"

"Since the carnival is over at eleven, I hope so."

"I was hoping I could see your Chevy turn into a pumpkin."

"Sorry to disappoint you. That won't be

happening and neither is me wearing glass slippers." Anne raised the flowing gown up a few inches to reveal her black corrective shoes.

Caleb leaned against one of the food booths, aware a few of the teens were setting some cakes and pies on the tables, but for some reason he found himself unable to take his attention from Anne. "I always wondered how a person could wear glass slippers."

"Delicately, I would imagine."

He chuckled. "So, why were you chasing this rabbit?"

"It got out of its pen. Billy has been looking for it, and I saw its furry tail sticking out from under this table so I came running. Found it sitting in the chair as if it were going to man the booth."

"Billy does have an array of animals for the kids tonight to enjoy. Half of them are his."

"They should keep some of the younger children occupied for, say, five whole minutes."

He responded to her comment with another laugh. Her wit appealed to him. "Here, let me take him. I don't want him to ruin that beautiful gown."

She placed the white rabbit into his hands,

and they started back across the gym toward the petting booth. "The doors should be opening soon."

Caleb scanned the large room. "Yes, and it looks like everything is ready. The kids really did get this pulled together."

"Was there any doubt?"

"Yes."

"Where's your faith?"

Her question brought him up short halfway across the gym. She stopped and faced him. "You know, you're right. I was totally discounting God in all this." Her gentle reminder that the Lord was with them erased what tension he had left. Tonight he would enjoy himself and not worry. He locked gazes with Anne, a constriction in his throat. "Thank you for reminding me what is important."

A shadow crept into her blue eyes. "I—I—you're welcome."

The rabbit squirmed in his arms, prompting him to move forward. "I think he's missing his buddies."

"He's a she and she's probably missing her babies."

"There are baby rabbits here?"

Anne nodded, gesturing toward the pen set up in the corner.

"They'll be a big hit with the children."

"Show time," Gina shouted from the entrance into the gym. The teenager caught sight of them and waved them over. "You two are needed in the photo ops room, also known as the arts-and-crafts room."

"We're working this evening?"

"So to speak. You'll be available for kids to take pictures with. Sorta like at Disney World."

As they headed for their assigned room, Caleb said, "I guess I'm glad I wasn't forced to wear a Goofy costume."

"That would have been priceless to see," Anne said with a laugh.

Again he discovered how much he liked listening to Anne's laughter. It reached inside him and touched a part of himself he hadn't realized was lonely.

"Too bad there isn't a ship behind us. Guys, we just have to make do with this old castle." Starlight Diner owner Sandra Lange, dressed as a pirate even down to the black head scarf and eye patch, moved her plastic sword out of the way and knelt down between Luke and Chance while Caleb snapped their picture.

"Tank you," each boy said, then kissed

Sandra on the cheek before running to their parents.

Meg scooped Luke up into her arms while Jared grabbed Chance and swung him high onto his shoulders. Every time Anne saw the family together her desire for one of her own grew, especially when she glimpsed the love shared among the four.

"Off to feed these rascals," Meg said, giving a check for the photo to Anne.

"We'll have the pictures ready next week." Anne stuffed the check into her money bag.

"You two have been stuck in this room for hours. I can take over and take a few pictures while you get something to eat," Sandra said, adjusting her eye patch.

"You're the main attraction with the kids," Anne said. "A pirate is much better than Cinderella and Prince Charming. At least with the boys."

Caleb changed the roll of film. "You didn't know you were gonna get roped into taking pictures, did you?"

"Nope. But I like it. It makes me feel like I'm doing something for the children." Sandra's eye got misty and she sniffled. "You two go. There's a timer on this camera so if anyone wants a picture with me I can set it and still take it. Wouldn't want to disappoint any of them." She straightened the scarf on her head. "Probably do me some good to move around a bit."

"If you're sure," Anne said, realizing when Meg had mentioned getting some food for the twins that she was hungry, too.

"Yeah. Besides, it's kinda slow right now." Sandra glanced around the empty room.

Caleb took Anne's hand and tugged her toward the door. "That's our cue to take a break. I could use one of those burgers Zach was eating."

She still wasn't used to Caleb's casual touch, and it took a few seconds for her brain to work so she could reply in an even voice. "Me, too. The aroma of cooking hamburgers has been driving me crazy for the past hour." Anne followed Caleb out into the hallway and passed Ross Van Zandt coming from the gym.

"Have either of you seen Sandra Lange?" the private investigator asked, dressed in what could only be considered a P.I.'s outfit from the 1940s—not exactly the fairy-tale theme of the night. Apparently he hadn't been able to bring himself to dress up in a *real* costume.

Caleb pointed toward the arts-and-crafts room. "She's in there."

Ross nodded his thanks and made his way into the room Caleb had indicated. He saw Sandra checking out a camera set up on a tripod. "It's good to see you here, Sandra."

She straightened from looking through the lens and smiled. "How's—" she scanned the room before continuing "—the investigation going? Any news?"

Ross, too, checked to make sure no one else was around to overhear what he had to say. He strode to within a foot of Sandra and lowered his voice, replying, "I've come up with one real good possibility so far. Ben Cavanaugh."

"Ben." The exhaustion in her expression faded as her green eyes lit with hope. "Yes, he's the right age."

"There are inconsistencies in his records with the adoption agency, but I must warn you there were a rash of children born nine months after that big snowstorm thirty-five years ago. There could be other possibilities beside Ben. I'm checking into some others, too."

Removing the eyepatch, Sandra lay her hand on Ross's arm, tears welling in her eyes. "I don't know how I can thank you for taking on this job. For years all I've thought about was my baby taken away from me at birth. I don't even know if I had a girl or a boy. Thank you, Ross." Wet tracks coursed down her cheeks.

He covered her hand with his large one. "Don't thank me until I've brought you the name of your child." He looked her in the eye. "And, Sandra, I will."

Chapter Six

"Job well done, Caleb." Gerald Morrow, the mayor of Chestnut Grove, patted Caleb on the back. "Our youth center is an exceptional program in our state. A model for others."

Caleb beamed. "Thank you." He surveyed the large crowd packed into the gym. "But it's support like this from the community that allows the center to keep improving."

"One of the platforms I'll be running on next year will be supporting our youth in Chestnut Grove. They're the foundation of our country."

Ducking her head, Anne rubbed her hand across her mouth to keep from smiling at the obvious campaign spiel that Gerald was already saying, even though he wouldn't be running for mayor for another year. He was an attractive older man with a full head of white hair. But there was something about him that bothered Anne. Perhaps his tough exterior. When she looked into his blue eyes as he was talking, she wondered about the hidden truths behind his words. It was apparent he was a man with an agenda, but there was also something else.

"There you are, darling." Lindsay Morrow, Gerald's wife, curled her arm through his and plastered herself against her husband's side. "It's good to see you, Caleb, Anne. Where are your parents, Anne? I haven't seen them lately."

"Out of town. I'm here representing the Smith family tonight."

"I'd hoped to see your mother. I caught her lecture on the American relationship with Eastern European countries after the Cold War. Very informative."

"Actually they are in New York City speaking before the United Nations."

"What an honor for both of them to be asked! I'll have to stop by and see your mother when she returns and give her my congratulations." Lindsay turned toward her husband. "Darling, I believe it's about time for us to announce the costume winners."

"Yes. Yes." Gerald strode away with his wife toward the stage at the north end of the gym.

"I guess since they were the judges, along with Gina and Jeremy, they decided not to wear a costume." Anne scanned the large room and noticed the Morrows were the only two adults without a costume on.

"Frankly I can't see Lindsay Morrow dressing up in any costume. Not her style." Caleb came closer to her. "Now what's this about your parents speaking before the United Nations? Why didn't you tell me?"

"I've been so busy lately I hadn't thought about it. My parents are always being asked to lecture at different functions." Those lectures had become more important to them than their own daughter. They lived for each other and their academic reputations. She'd always felt like an outsider in her own home.

"Mrs. Morrow is right. It's an honor for your parents."

"Yes, I'm sure it is," Anne said and stepped away, intending to put some distance between her and the direction the conversation was heading.

As people began to gather at the north end, someone jostled Anne and shoved her back into Caleb's side. Automatically he brought his hand up to steady her. She raised her gaze to his and for a long moment became lost in his eyes. Then a child darted through the mass, sending Caleb and Anne apart.

"That was Olivia. Which means Ben isn't too far behind her," Caleb said at the very second Ben weaved his way through the crowd. Caleb gestured to the left. "She went thataway."

"Thanks, Caleb." He headed off in pursuit.

"You know Olivia's wish for this Christmas is to have a mother to share it with."

"Who told you that?" Caleb asked, slipping his arm about Anne's shoulder.

"I can't remember, but I think it was Rachel, because she's her aunt now that she married Eli."

"At your Sunday brunch?"

"You know about that?"

"Who doesn't? You four have been meeting for years at the Starlight Diner after church services."

"The Four Musketeers."

"One for all and all for one, or some such thing."

"That's us." Anne thought back to her teenage years and realized without her three friends she might have run away from Chestnut Grove before graduating. With their support she had weathered the teasing and taunts by the other kids. Was that why Dylan's plight spoke to her on a deeper level than the others at the center?

"Ladies and gentlemen, it's that time we've all been waiting for, the announcement of the winners of the costume contest." Gerald's deep, booming voice blared through the gym with the help of the PA system.

A hush fell over the crowd with only one child whining that he was tired. Anne noticed it was Luke, and that Meg made her way through the crowd to the hallway with the two-year-old. Sandra and Ross came to the doorway of the gym to hear who had won.

"For the scariest costume, the prize goes to Zach Fletcher for his troll impersonation."

"Not too far a stretch," someone shouted out as Zach came up onto the stage for his prize, a chocolate cream pie from the Starlight Diner.

Zach hoisted the pie and said, "I'd be careful if I were you. I've got a weapon in my hands, and it's not police-issued." Chuckles followed the detective's departure from the stage.

Laughing, Gerald came forward with the microphone in his hand. "Be careful crossing the bridge going home tonight, folks. Now, for the next presentation. The winner of the funniest costume is Leah Paxson as the ugly duckling."

Leah waddled across the stage, throwing in a few quacks as she made her way toward Gerald for her pie. Children's giggles could be heard over the chattering in the crowd.

"And the last winner—or rather winners—are for the best couple costume. And who better than our very own Reverend Caleb Williams and Anne Smith, as Prince Charming and Cinderella."

"We won!" Anne exclaimed and threw her arms around Caleb for a second, until she realized what she had done. Quickly she backed away.

Grinning, he took her hand. "Let's get our pie."

Up on stage Anne stared out over the sea of people and gulped at all the faces turned her way. She couldn't remember a time when she had been in front of a crowd this size before. It wasn't something she would like to make a habit of, even if most of the faces were familiar ones.

"Sorry, you two. There's only one left. I guess you'll have to share." Gerald handed Caleb the last chocolate cream pie.

The townspeople applauded and each winner took a bow.

"We still have another hour, so everyone eat up and be merry." Gerald put the microphone on the podium. "Congratulations, y'all," he added before heading off stage.

Uncomfortable with being in the limelight, Anne quickly followed the mayor and nearly ran into Gerald and his wife whispering to each other backstage, frowns creasing their faces. "Excuse me." She dashed around them, aware of their silence now and the fact that Caleb was right behind her.

"Hold up, Anne."

"We should relieve Sandra." She paused by the stairs that led to the stage on the right side. "She's probably wondering where we've disappeared to."

"Fine. But you might slow down. I'd hate to drop our prize. My mouth's already watering in anticipation." He fell into step next to Anne. "We need to arrange a time to share this pie. Hey, I've got an idea. Why don't you come to the faith session tomorrow and then we can have a big piece of pie afterwards with a cup of coffee?"

"You mean a cup of tea?"

"No, but I guess for you tea it is." He stopped her before entering the arts-and-crafts room. "Well, how about it? Is it a date?"

A date? Had she heard right? Anne's heart skipped a beat, then began to slam against her rib cage. Her stomach flip-flopped and her mouth went dry.

"We can go to the Starlight Diner after the session. I'm sure Sandra won't mind since she made this pie in the first place if we brought our own dessert with us."

"I wouldn't mind at all," Sandra said from the doorway. "You two come tomorrow evening, and I'll even supply the coffee to go with the pie, my treat."

Caleb quirked an eyebrow at Anne. She saw the question in his expression, but for the life of her she was too stunned to reply to him. A date with Caleb!

"Anne, we can't disappoint Sandra, now can we?"

She shook her head. "No, we can't."

Caleb grinned. "Then we'll be at the diner tomorrow evening, Sandra, ready to devour this delicious pie."

"That's music to my ears." Sandra fluttered her hand toward the room. "The place is all yours. All this talk about pies has made me hungry."

Moving toward the castle backdrop, Caleb

said, "If you don't want to come tomorrow, I'll understand, Anne."

Had he already regretted his invitation, she wondered as he set their prize on a table along the wall.

"I don't want you to feel you have to come to one of the faith sessions to get your part of the pie." He pivoted toward her, an intense look in his eyes. "I want you to come because you want to find out about God. He has so much to offer, but I also realize forcing Him on someone doesn't work."

"I'd planned to come before the invitation. I want to bring Dylan if he and the Givens agree it's okay."

Caleb's serious expression melted into a smile. "That would be great!"

With his smile directed at her, all her doubts about his motives behind his invitation vanished. They were friends. Friends went out for pie and coffee, or tea in her case. She shouldn't read anything else into it.

He covered the space between them, taking hold of her hands. "Have you ever thought of being a foster parent?"

"Me!" The one word squeaked out while all her senses couldn't get past the fact that her crush held her hands and was only a foot from her.

"If anyone can get Dylan to come to the Sunday faith session, it will be you. I want to give the boy someone to believe in, a foundation to support him when he's going through rough times."

The space between them shrank even more. His scent surrounded her.

"He comes to church with the Givens, but I don't think he listens to what is being said. He hangs out here because they have allowed him to."

"Don't sell yourself short. I do think he's listening. But there's a lot of anger inside him. Until that's dealt with I don't know if he'll let anyone else in, including God."

"But God can take that anger away."

Another inch disappeared between them. "I'm not so sure the Lord can. Don't you think Dylan has to do it for himself?"

Caleb framed her face with his large hands, his fingers combing back into her hair. "You're never alone to fight your battles with God in your life."

The intensity of his regard tingled her lips. She ran her tongue across them, swallowing several times. "You keep telling me that."

"It's because it's the truth. I would never lie to you."

His fervent words robbed her of any coherent thought. Her mind went blank while her heartbeat pounded so loud she was sure he could even hear it. With his hands still cupping her face, his eyelids slid halfway closed as he brought his head toward hers.

"Hey, I was hoping it wasn't too late to get a picture taken," a voice said.

"Reverend Fraser, Naomi, there's always enough time for you two," Caleb said while he whipped away, recovering a lot faster than she did.

Anne closed her eyes as she stepped back, every muscle in her body going limp. She clutched the tripod to keep herself from collapsing from the sheer anticipation of Caleb's kiss that never came. Her heart still throbbed such a fast tempo that she heard its pulsating beat in her ears.

Even though Caleb was several feet away, taking the reverend's money for the photo, Anne could still smell his aftershave and the minty flavor of his toothpaste that laced his breath. She could still feel his fingers in her hair, molding her face as though she were something precious to behold.

With her usual pink uniform with ruffles and a fancy script "S" near her right shoulder, Sandra Lange approached the booth at the Starlight Diner with a beaming smile on her face, a contradiction to the exhaustion Anne saw in the woman's green eyes. She knew the older lady had been going through chemotherapy for her breast cancer and that her blond hair, always worn teased up, was cut very short and hidden under a blond wig.

"No more tea, Sandra," Anne said, placing her hand over her cup. "Brunch was delicious, as always. I'm stuffed."

Sandra looked her up and down. "Which isn't saying much. But you can make that up tonight when you have your slice of pie. I'll make it extra big. Put some meat on those bones." The Starlight Diner's owner then switched her attention to each of the other occupants of the booth. "The same goes for the rest of you. Y'all are going to blow away if a stiff wind comes through town. Thankfully I don't have that problem." She began clearing away the plates among grumbles from Pilar, Rachel and Meg, who protested her observation about her figure.

When Sandra left, Pilar asked, "Okay, Anne, what's she mean by tonight and a slice of pie? 'Fess up."

"I'm sharing the pie I won last night with Caleb here at the diner."

"A date?" Meg asked, leaning forward across from Anne.

Anne tilted her head and twirled the end of her hair, now too short to put in her usual ponytail. She had to wear it down and framed around her face, which had seemed odd today while she was getting ready to come to the diner for brunch with her friends. "I really don't know."

"Don't know? Either you are or you aren't." Rachel finished the last of her ice water.

"You tell me." Anne folded her arms on the table. "He invited me to come to the faith session he has on Sunday with the youths, then to come to the Starlight Diner and share our pie and a cup of coffee—or tea. So what do you call it?"

"A date. Definitely." Pilar put her napkin on the place mat.

Rachel and Meg agreed with nods.

"So what are you going to wear?" Rachel asked.

"What I have on." Anne waved her hand down the length of her, indicating her long black A-line skirt and white silk blouse. She wore a lot of black skirts and white blouses. This morning she'd counted four similar outfits in her closet. Maybe she should go shopping for something different.

"Have you heard of the word 'color'—like pink or teal blue? They would look good on you." Meg untied a turquoise scarf from around her neck. "Here. Try this."

"I don't need—"

Meg slid from the booth and placed the scarf around Anne's neck, securing it before sitting down across from her. "That does look good on you. Consider it a gift."

"But—"

Meg stopped Anne's words with a sharp look. "You know I like giving gifts to friends and we've been friends for a long time."

Anne touched the scarf. "Thank you."

"Promise us you'll call and tell us everything that happens tonight," Rachel said.

"Is it okay if I wait to call you until tomorrow?" Anne asked with a laugh, relishing her friendship with each one of them. They had been her anchor for so many years.

"I guess so. I'll probably be in bed early. Luke and Chance have been running me ragged lately. Twin toddlers are a handful."

"A job you're glad to have, Meg."

Anne realized the other three's lives were changing, and as Caleb mentioned, leaving her behind. They were wives now. Probably all three would soon be mothers, not just Meg.

Meg's pale blue eyes shone with love and pride. "Yeah. Wouldn't trade it for the world."

"Speaking of children, how are Gracie and Gabriel doing?" Anne asked, hoping to move the conversation away from her and her so called date this evening.

Rachel smiled. "Gracie is doing well, but I miss her now that Mom and Dad are home."

"Do you see her much?" Pilar asked.

"Every chance I get, but Eli and I hope to start our own family soon."

"Zach and I are looking at adopting." Pilar flipped her long black hair that had fallen behind her shoulders. "I sure miss Gabriel, too, but like you, Rachel, I get to see him. Ashley is wonderful about letting me visit."

Anne didn't know what she would have done if she had discovered an abandoned baby, cared for the child and then had him taken away as had happened to Pilar when they had found Gabriel's biological mother. Even though the Frasers had been Gabriel's foster parents, Anne had known how emotionally involved Pilar had become in the baby's life. That was why she didn't know if she could be a foster parent, as Caleb had suggested. She was afraid she would invest so much of herself in the child that when he was taken away, a part of her would go with him.

"God will provide for both of you. You all will be great mothers," Meg said, slipping from the booth. "Which reminds me, I'd better be heading home to my two little ones before they wake up from their naps."

Anne rose. "I need to leave, too. I'm going by to see if Dylan wants to come to the youth center with me."

"That poor child wasn't too happy last night following Brent and Mandy around at the carnival." Pilar scooted from the booth, opening her purse to withdraw her wallet. "I got the impression he was supposed to watch them the whole evening."

As Anne and her friends walked to the counter to pay their bills, she thought of the few times she had seen Dylan at the carnival. His face set in a frown, he'd trudged behind the two younger children as though he had been sentenced to prison and was dragging around a ball and chain. She might not be his foster parent but that didn't mean she couldn't give him the love she had inside her. He needed someone to care what happened to him.

Anne pulled up to the Givens' house, her hands locked in a death grip around the steering wheel. It was important to her to persuade Dylan to come to the faith session this afternoon. She wasn't even sure why she felt that way except, like herself, he was searching for answers. There was a chance what Caleb and the other youths had to say might lead to some.

Suddenly her grandmother's words came back to her. "The Bible says you can do all things through Christ, who strengthens you." Was that true? Wouldn't that be nice if it was?

The memory pried her fingers from the steering wheel and alleviated her tension. Grandma Rose had always made her feel better about herself. Her six-week visits every summer hadn't been long enough.

Climbing from her Chevy, Anne strode up to the Givens' front door and rang the bell. Cora answered, puzzlement on her face, a baby in her arms.

"Cora, I was heading to the youth center and wondered if Dylan would like to come."

Cora stepped back to allow her inside. "Dylan," she shouted up the stairs while patting the baby's back.

From the second floor the sound of crying could be heard.

"Patrick doesn't want to take his nap,"

Cora said, then ascended a few steps and shouted, "Dylan, you have a visitor."

A minute later the boy appeared at the top of the stairs, a sullen attitude slowing his progress. He saw Anne, and for a flash, she glimpsed surprise in his expression before he covered it with a frown. He trudged down the stairs.

"I thought you might like to come with me to the youth center. Caleb is meeting with some others about the challenges of their faith. From what I understand, anything you may have a question about is fair game."

"You staying?"

Anne nodded. The crying upstairs increased to screaming.

Dylan lifted one shoulder. "I guess so. I can't get anything done here." He pointedly looked up to the second floor landing before plodding toward the door.

"I'll have him home after the meeting," Anne said to the woman who was climbing the stairs.

As Anne left the house, she noticed Brent in the living room playing with a set of trucks on one end of the coffee table while Mandy colored on a piece of paper while kneeling at the other end. Brent, making the appropriate truck noises, drove a semi over Mandy's paper. The little girl leaped to her feet, snatching the truck from Brent. The child started crying. Mandy dashed from the room with the boy on her heels. Anne fled the chaotic household.

Outside on the porch the screaming lessened in intensity, but she jumped when she heard a door slam somewhere in the house. Searching for Dylan, she found him standing at the bottom of the steps.

"Just another fun day at the Givens'."

Such sarcasm from an eleven-year-old surprised Anne and sparked her need to reach Dylan somehow. "I grew up an only child so I'm not used to so much—noise." Anne descended to the sidewalk and started for her car. "I'm glad you decided to come with me."

"Why?"

She waited to respond until they were both in the car. As she turned the key in the ignition, she asked, "Do you believe in God?"

He blinked, surprise now showing on his face. "I—I—I don't know."

She pulled away from the curb. "That's the way I feel, too. I suspect that, like me, you have questions but have never asked them."

He slumped in the front seat. "Maybe."

"Well, Caleb assures me that these weekly

little get-togethers are a great place to ask those questions."

The boy snorted and sank farther down in the seat.

Anne remained silent the rest of the way to the youth center. Sometimes it was better not to say anything, but allow a person to consider what had been said. She felt this was one of those times. She hoped Dylan was thinking about a question he wanted answered. She had one.

At the center, the second she entered the TV room she sought Caleb, her gaze finding him sitting in a chair in front of the television. When he saw her, a smile graced his lips and twinkled in his eyes. Some of her discomfort quieted.

Caleb rose and came toward her. "It's good to see both of you here today. We'll be starting in a few minutes. Do you want to take a seat?"

Dylan scanned the others at the meeting, then selected a chair off by itself near the back.

Caleb put a hand on her arm to stop her from following the boy. "I'm glad you were able to get him to come."

Although he immediately released his hold on her, Anne missed the physical contact.

She liked being touched by Caleb, even casually. She'd grown up in a household where physical distance was kept—at least with her. There hadn't been many hugs from her parents, only her grandmother. "I thought after the meeting I'd take him home, then meet you at the diner."

"I've got a better suggestion. Why don't you and I take him home in my car, then after we eat, I can bring you back here for your car?"

"Fine," she murmured and continued on her way to where Dylan was sitting. The evening was definitely beginning to look more and more like a date.

When she dragged a chair over next to Dylan, she received a frown. "Since we're both new here, I thought we would keep each other company."

The boy grumbled something under his breath but kept his chair where it was.

Caleb began the meeting with a prayer asking for guidance in their journey of faith. Then he opened the meeting up to questions.

"I have a question," Anne said, and waited for Caleb to look her way before asking, "If God is the one true God who is all-powerful, then why are there so many religions in the world? He could make everyone believe in Him and Christ by using His power."

"That's a good question, Anne. Does anyone have an answer for her?" Caleb asked the group of teens.

"Free will," Gina said, facing Anne. "He has given us the right to make our own choices and that even includes if we are going to believe in Him."

"Jesus is God in the flesh," Caleb added. "No other religious leader claimed that divinity. Not Mohammed. Not Buddha. Christ is the one we must go through to get to God. Jesus said, 'I am the way and the truth and the life. No one comes to the Father except through me.'"

Caleb's answer prompted another question in Anne. "How do we know Christ is the son of God?"

Tiffany waved her hand in the air. "Jesus said He was. He told the high priest when he asked Him, knowing His answer would condemn Him."

"Yeah, and look at all the miracles Christ performed while He was alive," Jeremy added.

"His coming was predicted for hundreds of years and recorded in the Old Testament of the Bible. Every prophecy came true with

Jesus." Caleb rose, retrieved a black book from the table behind him and brought it to Anne. "Start by reading about Jesus's life in one of the gospels in the New Testament."

Anne took the Bible, her hands gripping it tightly as though it had all the answers inside it and she didn't want to let go. Perhaps it did have the answers she was looking for within its pages. She set it in her lap, intending to take Caleb up on his challenge.

The next half hour the youths discussed the different miracles that Jesus performed. Anne listened, occasionally watching Caleb, who said little but let the teens talk.

"Does God answer prayers today?" Caleb asked when there was a lull in the conversation.

Nikki straightened in her chair, leaning forward. "Yes, I prayed real hard for my baby brother to get well last year and he did. He's in remission."

Billy nodded. "I prayed for my grandfather not to die when he had that bad heart attack two years ago. He's doing great now."

Dylan shot to his feet, his arms rigid at his side. He shook with anger. Suddenly he spun around and raced for the door.

Chapter Seven

The slamming of the door behind Dylan reverberated through the TV room. Stunned, the kids fell silent. Anne rose and started after the boy.

"I think this is a good time to eat the cookies Tiffany's mom baked for us," Caleb announced, hurrying after Anne. "Tiffany, why don't you start passing them out?"

Out in the hall he caught up with her as she reached for the front door to the center. "Anne?"

She glanced back at him. "Let me talk to him first. Wait here."

He inclined his head and moved to the side while she opened the door and left. Fear clawed at her heart. The anger she had seen in the child's face tore at her composure and threatened to release the tears so close to the surface.

Dylan was perched on the edge of the steps, his head hanging down, his elbows on his knees, his hands loosely clasped between his legs. Anne eased down beside him, but like the time before when she had caught him crying in the TV room, she remained quiet, letting him control the conversation.

"If there is a God like they believe in there, then why do bad things happen to good people?" His voice resonated anger.

"Who are you talking about?" Anne asked, knowing the answer to her question would be important in discovering what was really bothering the child.

His mouth firmed into a frown, his shoulders hunching even more as though the boy were curling in on himself. "My mom. She died two years ago and—" Dylan sucked in a shaky breath.

Anne couldn't keep her distance any longer. Even if Dylan pulled away, she had to comfort him the best way she knew. She slipped her arm about his shoulders and hugged him to her side. "What happened?" she asked in a gentle voice, meant to soothe the hurt, if only for a little while.

Again he drew in a breath that rasped,

twisting his hands together. "She tried to save a child from drowning even though she couldn't swim very well. She drowned."

All the heartache that Anne had endured was nothing compared to what Dylan had gone through in his short life. *What do I say to him, Lord?* Shocked by the question that flitted through her mind, she nearly released Dylan.

"Why did God take her away? She believed in Him. Went to church every Sunday."

Dylan's raw words lay bare the inadequacies Anne felt answering a question about faith in the Lord. And yet, she wished she could. She glanced over her shoulder toward the door into the center, hoping that Caleb was visible. He was. Relieved, she motioned to him to join them.

Caleb came to sit next to Dylan on the other side. He didn't say anything for a long moment, waiting for the child to talk first. When Dylan didn't, Caleb captured Anne's attention, a question in his expression.

"Why do bad things happen to good people who believe in God? Why doesn't their faith protect them against bad things?" She wanted to know the answer, too. Anne ran her hand up and down Dylan's arm, wishing she could infuse her warmth into his chilled body.

"Believing in the Lord doesn't guarantee a person a good life here on earth, only an everlasting one in Heaven with God when he or she dies."

"But I needed my mom." Tears flowed down Dylan's cheeks as he drew further in on himself.

Caleb squatted in front of him, his presence compelling the boy to look at him. "I can't begin to second-guess God in what He has planned for you, but when you believe in the Lord, you are never alone even when it seems the darkest. One of my favorite Bible verses is, 'I am with you always, to the very end of the age.'"

Dylan looked up at Caleb. "You think Mom is with God now?"

He nodded.

"But everything changed after she died. She protected me."

"From who?" Anne asked, her heart feeling as if it were being squeezed in a vise.

Dylan immediately dropped his head way down so no one could see his face.

"Dylan, who?" Caleb asked, placing his hand over the boy's clasped ones.

"My father. After she died, I couldn't—" Dylan swallowed hard. "I couldn't hide. He always found me."

"Dylan, what happened?" Anne kept her arm about him, wishing she could do more to comfort the child.

"He liked to hit me." Dylan lifted his head. "But only when he was drinking. If he stops, I can go back."

"Is that what you want?" Caleb asked.

"Yes—no—I don't know. I—" Tears continued to streak down Dylan's face. "I'm tired. I want to go ho—to the Givens' house."

Caleb rose. "Let me see if Reverend Fraser can come over and take care of the group. I see his car is still at the church. Then Anne and I will drive you home."

Caleb was halfway down the steps when Dylan asked him, "Did you really apply to be a foster parent because of me?"

"Yes."

Since the incident with Dylan had occurred, Anne purposely hadn't said anything about the boy and what he had revealed to Caleb. On the drive over to the Starlight Diner from the Givens' after dropping Dylan off, Caleb hadn't spoken, but his brow had knitted as though he was deep in thought.

Over a spaghetti dinner, Anne had steered the conversation to the success of the fall carnival.

Now Anne realized it was time to discuss Dylan. She took a sip of her hot tea, then said, "We should talk about what happened earlier."

"I know." Noticing Sandra heading toward their booth, he clamped his mouth closed.

The older woman placed a piece of their prize pie in front of Anne and Caleb. "I've boxed up the rest separately for y'all to take home. Enjoy."

"We will." Anne picked up her fork and slid it into her piece. "This has got to be the best of all the pies you make."

"Thank you, sugar. A cook appreciates that and I do love to make pies." Sandra hurried off.

Anne slipped the bite into her mouth. Delicious. "Now this is worth going off my diet."

With his mouth full Caleb nodded his agreement. "If you want me to take your half of the leftovers, I'll sacrifice my waistline in order to help you."

Anne laughed. "I wouldn't want you to do that. That wouldn't be fair to you. No, I'll eat every last bite of my half."

The creases at the sides of his eyes deepened. He tasted his pie again. "Mmm."

Two minutes later Anne finished the last of her dessert, not a crumb left. She washed it down with a large swallow of her lukewarm tea. "Now that we have gotten that out of the way, we need to talk about Dylan."

"Yes. What he told me this evening makes me even more determined to become his foster parent. He needs stability and love."

"He certainly hasn't had it. Having to hide from your father so he won't hit you." Anne shivered at the thought. "My parents aren't very loving, but they have never physically harmed me."

"As I suspected, his father leaving him alone for several days wasn't the only reason he was taken from the home."

"No wonder Dylan is so angry."

Caleb pushed his empty plate to the side and leaned his elbows on the table. "So what do we do about it?"

"Show him another side to life. Do some fun activities with him."

"How about next Saturday night we take him to a movie and then pizza afterwards?"

We. Anne liked the sound of that. She could help Dylan and be with Caleb on a Saturday night—as if they were dating, a real couple.

"Do you think his foster parents will go for it?"

"Are you kidding? Cora looked like she was ready to throw in the towel dealing with Patrick today. I think one less child will be a welcome relief."

"Which is sad for Dylan. If we see that, then you know he does."

"Yeah, I know. He's a smart kid."

Caleb drank the last of his coffee, then pulled the check toward him.

Were they on an official date? She really didn't know, especially since she wasn't very apt at this dating. She felt like the proverbial bull in the middle of a china shop. "How much do I owe you for my dinner?"

Caleb's eyes widened for a second before a frown descended. "Not a thing. This was my treat."

By the tight look on his face Anne could tell she had upset him by asking. She bit down on the inside of her cheek to keep from saying anything else. His expression only reinforced her earlier assessment—she wasn't very good at this dating thing. She would chalk it up to her overloaded mind. So much had happened today. Even though knowing Dylan's full story saddened her, she was glad he had finally said something to her and that

Caleb could give him answers concerning the Lord.

Fingering the Bible next to her on the seat, Anne knew when she went home, she would spend some time reading one of the gospels as Caleb had suggested. The youth meeting had sparked a desire to know more. Because Grandma Rose believed, as well as Caleb, she wanted to believe, to see why someone like Caleb unquestionably believed in God. But wanting and believing were two different things.

After Caleb had paid the bill, he escorted her to his Suburban. "I'll pick you up at your house on Wednesday at five-thirty. That should give us enough time to get to the hospital."

"That's fine."

"I can't wait to hold one of those babies again." Caleb opened the passenger side of the car to allow her inside.

"I can't either. I missed not going last week. I need my baby fix."

Cradling a baby boy to his chest while feeding him with a bottle, Caleb watched Anne doing the same thing except with a tiny premature girl whose mother had been on drugs even while she had been pregnant. Listening to Anne talking softly to the child wrenched his heart. Anne was such a good person. *Why doesn't she believe in You, Lord? I'm doing everything I can, but still I feel a resistance on her part. Please, Heavenly Father, help me. I need her to believe.*

The desperation in his last sentence took him by surprise. He was scared he was falling in love with Anne and just as scared he was going to end up with a broken heart.

"She's so adorable. Her mother hasn't even given her a name yet."

Caleb heard the cracking in Anne's voice and knew she was close to tears. What a wonderful mother she would make. For a second he pictured her holding their baby and panic zipped through him. He couldn't allow his heart to go there. From past experience he knew what disaster lay in that thinking.

"From what the nurse said she'll be here a while." Anne looked up into his eyes. "She's underweight, not to mention having a myriad of problems because of the drugs her mother took while carrying her. I hope she has a name the next time we come."

We. He liked the sound of that. He liked sharing this with Anne. He liked being with her. The big question was, could he continue to be with her and not want their relationship to develop into love? He was fighting the urge more and more lately and he was afraid one day he would give in, which would only mean they would both end up deeply hurt. He didn't want to do that to Anne. He had to be the strong one.

"If not, I'm gonna give her a name, just between her and me."

Anne's smile as she stared down at the child held such sadness that Caleb's throat contracted. "What would you name her if you could?"

"Rose, after my grandmother. She was such a warm, loving woman. Beautiful inside and out."

Like you, Caleb thought, placing the bottle down so he could pat his baby's back. "Then Rose it is. Like the flower, I pray this child grows tall, opens up and blossoms beneath the sunshine."

Anne paused in rocking, snagging his gaze. "Rose and I like how you put that."

"You do?"

She resumed rocking the baby. "Yep. If you ever decide to give up being a youth minister maybe you could write lyrics for songs or even poems."

He chuckled. "That will be the day."

"That you write songs or give up being a youth minister?"

"Both. I love what I do. I can't see doing anything else. To work with young people and serve God at the same time surpasses holding babies and that says a lot because I'm really enjoying holding this little one." Caleb peered at the child in his arms who had fallen asleep.

"It must be wonderful to feel that way about your job."

"You don't?"

Both eyebrows shot up. "No. I work with a bunch of numbers all day. How wonderful can that be? It's a job I'm good at, but that is all. That's why I volunteer to hold babies." The second she had said that to Caleb, surprise at her answer dominated her thoughts. Where had those feelings come from? Her job had always seemed enough in the past. But in the last few weeks she had glimpsed something more.

"Have you considered changing jobs? Doing something entirely different?"

"Like what?" Up until a few minutes ago, she hadn't even realized she wasn't satisfied with what she was doing.

He shrugged. "Oh, I don't know..." He peered at the ceiling then after a long moment directly at her. "What about working with children? You love holding babies."

"Working with children?" Being constantly around other people? Anne wasn't sure she was ready for that. One of the pluses of her job was that she was in her office working by herself most of the day, not required to work too much with others. Was that changing about her, too? "What would I do?"

"We could still use a volunteer at the day-care at the church on Sunday. Why don't you start there and see where it leads you?"

Anne chewed on her bottom lip.

"Give it a shot. We can always use an extra pair of hands in the nursery."

"Okay," Anne said slowly, unsure if this was right for her but willing to give it a try. She didn't see her own family in her future at the moment so maybe this was the next best thing—looking after other children like holding these babies.

Caleb grinned. "You won't regret it."

His expression melted her heart and made her all mushy inside. "I think you're right. How can you regret working with children?"

"Have you ever thought of becoming a teacher?"

The question brought her up short. Teacher? "I—I don't know if I could do that." Standing in a room full of thirty children all looking at her, hanging on her every word, following her every move.

"I thought I saw you two in here," Eli Cavanaugh said from the doorway, bringing up his scarred left hand, to hang his stethoscope around his neck. "Did Anne recruit you to be a baby holder?"

"Yes and I'm thankful she did." Caleb rose from the rocking chair to give his baby to the nurse.

Anne stood, too. "This is late for even you. Heading home?"

Eli's features transformed with a wide smile. "Yes. Rachel's holding dinner for me. I had to check on a patient one more time. Thankfully he's doing better. Are you leaving?"

"Yeah. Our time is up." Anne transferred her baby to the nurse's embrace, already feeling the emptiness in her arms. She always hated this part, giving the babies back.

"I'll walk you out to the parking lot." Eli waited by the door.

As Anne strode by the large window that afforded people a view of the babies, she paused and looked at the bassinets. The longing for her own child grew in her heart. At that moment Caleb laid his hand on her shoulder and squeezed gently as though he could tell what she was feeling, perhaps even experiencing the same emotions. She felt connected to him as never before and knew the danger in that. She was going to get hurt.

The soft glow of her porch light illuminated Caleb's handsome face, reminding Anne again that she was dreaming if she thought their relationship went beyond friendship. Even knowing that, she hated for the evening to end. Sharing her time with the babies with Caleb had strengthened her bond with him and she wanted time to explore that further.

"Thanks for the taco salad," Anne said, the cool, fall breeze whipping strands of her hair about.

"Fast food was invented for people on the go and we certainly were that tonight. Until coming back to Chestnut Grove this evening after the hospital, I'd forgotten all about having not eaten dinner." He glanced down at his watch. "And here it is nearly nine o'clock. Good thing you saw that restaurant because I have nothing in my refrigerator."

Anne pressed back against her front door.

"I would have taken pity on you and fixed you something to eat before you went home. In fact, would you like a cup of decaf coffee?"

Both of his eyebrows rose. "You'd fix me coffee when you don't drink it?"

"Yes. My parents drink it and we have all the necessary equipment."

"Sure, I would like some."

Glad their evening together wasn't over, Anne unlocked the door and headed straight for the kitchen with Caleb right behind her. She quickly put the coffee on to brew while she turned the kettle on to boil some water for her tea.

Caleb made a full circle around the kitchen as though he was too restless to sit. Stopping in front of a painting over the desk in the corner, he studied it for a moment. Anne's heartbeat increased, the temperature in the room soaring.

"This is really good. I love the field of wildflowers. I feel like I'm standing in the middle, experiencing all the colors, feeling the wind blowing, the sun shining. Where did your parents get this?"

He liked it! Relief trembled through Anne. "I painted it."

Caleb spun around to face her. "You did?

I didn't know you painted. You're good. Why didn't you say anything to me?"

Anne ducked her head and turned toward the counter where the coffee dripped into the glass pot. "Not many people know that about me. It's something I've always done in private to—" The words to complete her sentence couldn't get past the lump in her throat.

"To what?" Caleb asked, standing now right behind her.

She gripped the edge of the counter, part of her wishing she hadn't said she'd painted the picture. How did she explain to him all her passion for life and her emotions went into her paintings?

"Anne?" His hand touched her shoulder.

She drew in a deep, composing breath and slowly faced Caleb. "I've always been a very private person, shy, reserved. With my painting I'm not. All my feelings are conveyed when I stand before a canvas with my paintbrush." There, she had told him something she hadn't told another, not even Pilar, Rachel or Meg. She flicked her hand toward the picture on the wall above the desk. "The particular day when I painted that was right after I had come back from my first time volunteering to hold the babies at the hospital."

Caleb swung around and stared at the

painting. "You've captured the feelings so well. That's how I felt tonight—still do. Jubilant. Elated that life could be so good. You should share your talent."

She could never show others her work because she couldn't deal with the rejection if they didn't like her pictures. Art was so subjective. "I paint for myself, not others. The only reason this painting is hanging down here was that my mother insisted on putting it up because the colors matched her kitchen wallpaper. I couldn't tell her no." *Because she'd never expressed any kind of interest in me or my paintings,* Anne added silently.

"So you have other paintings?"

She nodded.

"May I see them?" When she didn't say anything immediately, he quickly added, "I'll understand if you tell me no."

She busied herself pouring the coffee for Caleb, then preparing her cup of tea, not sure how to answer him. She didn't know if she could let him in that much.

"Never mind, Anne. I shouldn't have asked. That wasn't fair. Just know if you ever want to show me your work, I would feel honored."

Cradling the cup of tea in her hands to

warm the sudden chill that encompassed her, she said, "Let's go sit in the living room."

Seated on the maroon couch, Caleb took a sip of his coffee before putting it down on a glass coaster on the end table next to him. "About Saturday. I've had second thoughts about it since we talked Sunday evening."

Anne's hand tightened around her cup. She felt as though she was waiting for the other shoe to fall.

"I would rather us spend all day together with Dylan and go some place like Jamestown or Williamsburg. What do you say about making it an all-day outing?"

With her hand quivering, Anne put her cup on a coaster and relaxed at the other end of the couch. "Jamestown. Williamsburg. I haven't been to either place since I was a little girl. I think it would be fun."

"Great! I'll talk to Dylan and Rex Givens tomorrow and let you know if it's a go for Saturday. We'll get an early start."

"Is Dylan opening up any more in counseling?"

"A little. He's had to be tough for so long it's hard for him not to be."

"We learn patterns early in life and it's not easy to break them." She was a good example of that!

"I agree, but a person can change if he wants. It all depends on the motivation behind the desire to change."

"Have you ever wanted to be someone different?" she asked, realizing she was asking a question that could open a door she wished would remain closed.

"No. How about you?"

"Yes." *Many times,* she silently added, not brave enough to say it out loud.

"Who do you want to be that you aren't?"

Beautiful, accomplished, outgoing, charming, she thought but again she couldn't voice those traits. "I wish I wasn't so shy," she answered, settling on a small part of the whole.

Caleb angled around so he was facing her on the couch. "How do you see yourself?"

"Shy, quiet, hardworking."

"Do you know how I see you? Beautiful, warm, caring with a quiet wit."

"You do? Beautiful has never been used to describe me," she said, latching onto the first word in his description.

"There's more to the word beautiful than what a person sees with his eye. I do think you are beautiful physically but also inside. I've seen a woman who cares enough about a little boy that she has reached out to him. I've seen a woman who volunteers two evenings a week to hold babies because they need her love. I've seen a woman take some teenage girls under her wing and make them work as a team."

Anne brought a hand up to touch her hot cheek. She'd never felt more womanly than in that moment. Caleb's words caused her heart to soar, and it felt as if she were floating on air. "All my life I have felt less than perfect."

"Who's perfect? Jesus was the only one who roamed this Earth who was perfect. Everyone else is less than perfect. I don't even want to tell you all the mistakes I've made."

"What?" she asked, aware that one word held a challenge.

He glanced away for a long moment. When he reestablished eye contact, sadness enveloped him. "When I was growing up, I had a good friend who was being physically abused by his father. I didn't see the signs or maybe I could have stopped him from killing himself. I should have been there for him. I should have done something."

"How old were you?"

"I was thirteen when he killed himself. In his note he said he couldn't take it anymore. That day he had given me some baseball cards that he treasured. I didn't realize he was giving away all his prized possessions because he knew he was going to end his life. I was just so happy to have the cards I'd always wanted. If only I—" Caleb's words came to a shaky halt. He sucked in a raspy breath. "I haven't talked about this in a long time. I don't talk about this. See the power you have, Anne?"

Power? Her? Anne never had thought of herself like that. But this man was causing her to reassess herself.

"It's always easy to look back and see what we could have done differently. It's not that easy to see that while we're living it, however. I could tell you not to beat yourself up over what happened to your friend but I'm not. You already know that in here." Anne reached out and grazed her fingertips across his forehead. "It's in here," she touched his chest over his heart, "that you need to realize it. Until you do, you won't have a resolution."

Scooting closer, Caleb captured her hand that brushed his chest and held it between them. "You're right. With God's help I will one day. I should add to my description of you that you are very wise, Anne Smith."

She found herself leaning toward Caleb as

though he were a source of light that she was desperately seeking. He lifted his free hand and cupped the side of her face.

"Anne, what's going on here?"

The sound of her father's voice boomed through the quiet of the living room. Anne tugged her hand from Caleb's grasp and turned to find her parents standing in the entrance into the living room.

Chapter Eight

"Mom! Dad! You're back a day early." Anne shot to her feet, red patches blossoming on her cheeks.

Caleb rose, feeling the tension in the room escalating. He stood behind Anne and desperately wanted to place his hands on her shoulders to convey his support. But the glare he received from Anne's father halted the impulse.

"Yes, well, we were tired of living out of a suitcase and decided to come home early." A distinguished looking woman in a suit with her gray hair pulled back into a severe bun came into the room, extending her hand toward Caleb. "I'm Anne's mother, Dr. Sarah Smith."

Caleb stepped to Anne's side and took her mother's hand. "I'm Caleb Williams."

"Aren't you the minister at the youth center?" The older gentleman finally moved forward.

"Yes, sir."

Anne's father's frown deepened, if that were possible. His heavy brows drew together and he didn't extend his hand to shake with Caleb. The air chilled. He didn't have to have a neon sign blinking, "You are not welcome here," to know her parents were not happy to meet him.

Caleb turned toward Anne. "I'd better be going. I'll call you about Saturday." He briefly grasped Anne's hand before making his way past her father and toward the front door.

Caleb heard light footsteps behind him and glanced back. Anne rushed toward him, regret visible in her expression. He smiled.

"I'm sorry," she whispered.

"What about?"

"My parents. They don't usually act that way. I mean, they aren't really warm people, but they were downright hostile. I don't understand."

Caleb couldn't resist. He brushed his fingers down her jaw. "I think I do."

"Because you're a minister. I suppose you're right. They don't understand why people believe in a god. They believe in the power of the human race, nothing more or less."

"I'll see you Saturday. We'll leave early."

Caleb left, hearing the closing of the front door as though it echoed through his mind. Anne didn't realize what he had—that her father had seen him as a potential suitor and hadn't liked it. Caleb dropped his head and massaged the back of his neck. He was tired. From the long day, but mostly from fighting the feelings developing for Anne. Being strong took a lot of energy.

He descended the steps and stared up at the clear, crisp fall night. Hundreds of stars shone and a half moon was low on the horizon. *What am I going to do, Lord? I don't want to fall in love with Anne and have to walk away.*

"I liked the ship and the fort," Dylan said, walking between Anne and Caleb toward the Memorial Cross at Jamestown. "But I'm glad I live now."

Anne laughed. "So am I. Just cleaning the clothes and making the meals were a big chore. I have to admit I enjoyed trying my hand at some of the everyday activities, though. Made me appreciate what we have."

Caleb stopped before the large wooden

cross erected to commemorate the first settlers at Jamestown. "The colonists were buried along that ridge almost four hundred years ago." He pointed toward the area. "That's the earliest English burial ground."

"Cool." Dylan went toward the ridge.

Anne sat on the steps leading up to the Memorial Cross and peered up. Not a cloud could be seen. A light, cool breeze blew off the James River, bringing with it a dank, fishy smell. The vivid, clear blue of the sky rivaled the still green trees near the cross.

"We couldn't have picked a better day," Caleb said as he settled on the step next to her, stretching out his long legs, clad in jeans. "The temperature is a perfect seventy-two."

"And Dylan seems to be really enjoying himself."

"I thought it was touch-and-go there for the first hour or so, but once he was able to explore the replica of one of the Jamestown ships, he forgot to be angry."

"It was fun, but no way would I have sailed on one of those across the Atlantic. It was dark and cramped."

An airplane soared above them. Caleb followed its path until it disappeared from view. "I wonder what the colonists would have thought of a plane."

"They probably would think we were crazy to ever step into one."

"I'm thinking they definitely would think we were crazy. Sometimes I think we are."

There was so much she didn't know about Caleb. She hoped today she could change that. "Are you afraid of flying?"

"I don't mind turning control over to God, but not to an unknown pilot of a plane."

"But aren't you really turning your life over to God when you fly?"

"When it's your time to die, it's your time?"

"Yes."

"I suppose you're right. I hadn't thought of it that way. So I shouldn't be afraid of anything then?"

"Yes." Anne stared at Caleb, her hand shielding her eyes from the glare of the sun. "But fear keeps us from doing stupid things."

"True, and this conversation is getting too deep for me."

Caleb chuckled. "I get the hint. Only fun and light conversation today."

At that moment her stomach rumbled. She patted it and grinned. "I guess I'm hungry. Where are we going next?"

"Williamsburg. I realize it's a lot to do in

one day, but I wanted you two to get a taste of both places."

Anne leaned away from him, looking him directly in the eye. "Are you a history buff?"

He inclined his head. "You've discovered my secret."

"What time period do you like the best?"

With arms straight behind him, he propped himself up and gazed at the sky. "Let's see. I like Roman history the best, followed closely by the American Revolutionary period."

"Those times are quite different. Why Roman history?"

"Christianity was born during the time that Rome dominated the world. It's interesting to study the climate of the times—and I don't mean weather patterns."

"You mean people and their beliefs."

He nodded, even though she hadn't really asked a question. "What do you like to do other than paint and add numbers?"

Anne averted her gaze, clasping her hands together. "I like to read."

"What?"

She groaned. She'd known he was going to ask that. "Romances."

"Ah. Are you a closet romantic?"

She lifted her chin and directed her regard

to him. "I like stories that have happy endings." Inwardly she winced at the defensive tone of her voice.

He held up the flats of his palms. "I do, too. But I have to admit I don't read romances, only the Bible and nonfiction books about history, which don't always have happy endings."

"Well, if more men would read romances, they might get an idea of how to treat women." The second she said that, she clasped her hand over her mouth, surprised she had voiced that opinion out loud. But Caleb had a way of making her open up when she rarely did with others.

"So you think men need lessons in how to treat women right?"

She looked away, her hands twisting together. "Some do."

"Do I?"

There was no humor in his question. She only heard sincerity, and when she slanted a glance toward him, she saw that same emotion visible in his expression. She didn't know how to answer him because they really weren't a couple. "You're a good friend," she finally said, pleased at her answer.

"Is that all?"

His question caused her mouth to drop

open. Quickly she closed it, her teeth digging into her lower lip. Her eyes must be as big as saucers. For a few precious seconds the rest of the world vanished, leaving only Caleb and her. A shriek of a bird flying overhead broke the spell.

Blinking, he waved his hand. "Forget I asked that."

But she couldn't forget the question. It burned in her mind with all kinds of possibilities. What would it be like to be more than friends with Caleb? What would it be like if he kissed her?

Dylan ran up to them. "I'm hungry, guys. Can we go get something to eat?"

Caleb surged to his feet, then extended a hand to help Anne up. She fit hers in his grasp and let him pull her up. He kept his hand about hers as they started for the car.

"Any suggestions where to eat?" Caleb asked Dylan.

"Somewhere we can get a hamburger."

"Sounds good to me. How about you, Anne?"

She was aware that Caleb had asked her an important question, but her whole attention was focused on the fact they were holding hands as they walked to the car. Like a couple.

"Anne?"

Her name brought her back to the present. "Hamburgers? Sure, I love them."

"Good. Then we'll find a place that serves thick, juicy ones before we head to Williamsburg."

"We're not going back to Chestnut Grove?" Dylan slipped into the back of the Suburban.

Caleb released Anne's hand and opened the door for her. "No, not until this evening unless you want to go home after we eat."

"No!"

Anne snapped out of her dazed state and turned to look at Dylan. "Caleb is a bit of a history buff."

While Caleb rounded the front of the car, Dylan said, "I kinda figured that out back at the fort when he read everything there was to read. Did you see all the information sheets and pamphlets he gathered?"

Anne grinned. "You're one smart kid."

Dylan puffed out his chest and returned her smile.

Anne listened to the rat-a-tat of the drums and the lively tune of the fifes as the corps marched by. Tapping her foot, she noticed Dylan's rapt attention as he stood between her and Caleb at the Governor's Palace in Williamsburg.

When the performance was over, he said, "There are kids my age playing."

"A corps back two hundred fifty years ago was usually made up of boys ten to eighteen. But since this is the twenty-first century there are boys and girls in this corps." Caleb headed toward the entrance into the Governor's Palace.

"He's a walking history book," Dylan said with a laugh.

Anne loved hearing the boy laughing and seeing him smile. After a rushed lunch Caleb had whisked them to Williamsburg in time to observe the Fifes and Drums Corps perform. She still marveled at all they had seen so far.

As she entered the palace, she asked Caleb, "Have you been here before?"

"Many times. I love colonial history and this is one of the best places to experience it. Don't you feel like you've stepped back in time?"

Dylan stared at the high ceiling as he made a slow circle, his mouth hanging open. "This is awesome!"

Anne agreed with Dylan. The entryway was unusual with a sense of power being conveyed from the ceiling with the circle of bayonet-tipped muskets, to the walls with swords mounted on them.

Caleb whispered close to Anne's ear, "I think I have a convert. Wait till I get him to Washington, D.C." He grabbed her hand and pulled her along with him to the parlor, Dylan trailing behind them, his eyes round.

Thirty minutes later Anne emerged from the palace to gaze at the formal gardens behind the building. The day was still perfect with the temperature rising maybe a few degrees. A light breeze brushed across her and sent stray strands of hair across her face.

"There's the maze I promised you," Caleb said to Dylan, pointing toward the back of the garden.

Dylan raced toward the tall green hedges that formed a labyrinth. "See if you can find me." He disappeared inside the maze.

Not releasing his hold on her hand, Caleb headed after Dylan. The child's laughter could be heard from deep within the live puzzle.

As the green walls enclosed about Anne, she began to feel tense. She halted a few feet inside. "Maybe I should wait out here for Dylan."

Caleb glanced back at her, dropping her hand so it fell to her side as he edged closer to her. "Is something wrong?"

"I'm a little claustrophobic."

"Anne? Caleb? Where are you?"

"Coming," Caleb shouted to Dylan, then to Anne he asked, "Are you sure you don't want to come? I'll be with you. It's fun."

Anne was not totally convinced it would be fun, but when she stared at the dancing gleam in Caleb's eyes, she couldn't resist the invitation. She moved forward, hoping she didn't regret going into the maze. He made her feel safe. He made her feel as though she could do anything. He took her hand again and hurried along the path deeper into the labyrinth.

"Anne? Caleb? Where-oh-where are you?"

Dylan's singsong voice calmed some of the panic nibbling at her defenses. She didn't want to spoil the boy's fun, and Caleb was with her. The strong feel of his fingers about hers strengthened her resolve that she wouldn't allow a little fear to ruin the day.

But as she followed Caleb, her heart beat rapidly in contrast to the slow pace of her steps. When she looked up, all she saw was blue sky with one wispy white cloud—oh, yes, and high green walls everywhere.

Rounding a bend in the hedge, Dylan jumped out and Anne gasped, bringing her loose hand up to cover her heart that thudded so loud she wondered if Caleb could hear it.

The boy took one look at her—she was sure her face had gone completely white like the cloud above—and quickly said, "I'm sorry. I didn't mean to scare you, Anne."

"You and Caleb are getting to be pros at that."

Caleb laid his hand on Dylan's shoulder. "She has this thing about people surprising her. We're supposed to whistle as we approach."

"Oh, I'll remember that."

Anne wasn't so sure he would if his impish grin was any indication. "Get me out of here. I think I've had enough mazes for one day. Where to next, tour guide?"

"We can stroll down the Duke of Gloucester Street and visit some of the shops."

"What kind of name is that for a street?" Dylan screwed his face into a puzzled look.

"An old name. It was named that in 1699 after William, Duke of Gloucester. Some very famous people have strolled where we are going to. Patrick Henry, Thomas Jefferson, George Washington, James Madison."

Beneath the shade of the large trees they walked the length of the street, stopping at several of the shops to browse.

"Look at that sign," Dylan said, fascinated with the different ones that displayed what the stores were. "I understand a pig on the grocer's sign, but why a ship on Greenhow General Provisions?"

"Probably because so many of their provisions came from England by ship," Caleb answered, smiling at Anne.

For a few seconds she imagined them as a family, enjoying a vacation away from home. She imagined Caleb having eyes for only her. She imagined Dylan as their child. Suddenly she put a halt to her thoughts, realizing almost too late the danger in those dreams. She and Caleb were only friends. She had to keep telling herself that. She was so afraid she was setting herself up to be really hurt.

"Hey, look here. What's an apoth—" Dylan peered at Caleb for help.

"An apothecary is what we would call a pharmacy today. Want to go in?" Dylan was inside the shop before Caleb had finished his sentence. "I guess he does." Outside he paused and faced Anne. "Are you enjoying yourself?"

She nodded.

"You aren't too mad at me for making you go into the maze?"

The boyish grin on his face nearly undid her composure. All the dreams came rushing back at once, and she quickly had to cut them off. "No, but we'd better go in before Dylan gets into something he shouldn't."

In the shop a lady dressed in a blue gown with white trim from the eighteenth century and a white cap covering her hair greeted them. Anne stood back while the woman explained about the apothecary to Caleb and Dylan, both engrossed in what she said while Anne was enthralled by the expressions on the guys' faces. If Caleb became Dylan's foster parent, and she couldn't see why he wouldn't, then those two were going to enjoy themselves exploring the various historical places in and around Virginia.

Maybe they would ask her to accompany them every once and a while, she thought with a wistful sigh.

"Ready for our last treat before we have dinner and head back to Chestnut Grove?" Caleb asked when they left the Pasteur and Galt Apothecary Shop.

"What?" Dylan shifted from one foot to the other as though he couldn't contain his energy.

"Let's take a ride in a carriage just like they would have traveled two hundred years ago."

Dylan bounced up and down. "Yes!"

When they were settled in the carriage,

Dylan sat between them, craning his neck in both directions to see everything. Anne relaxed back, exhaustion beginning to take hold. It had been a long day of excitement and fun. She couldn't remember having such a good time in—she couldn't remember how long ago, if ever she'd had such a good time. Peacefulness blanketed her as they passed by the different shops and houses—red brick, white wooden siding, moss on the roofs of some structures, dormer windows. She could almost imagine herself in another time.

When the carriage ride ended, Caleb hurried them to the Shields Tavern for colonial style dining. Anne felt as though she had stepped back into the 1750s with its historically accurate decor. The tavern oozed warmth and country living.

"Order anything you want," Caleb said as he sat next to her at the table. "I hear these recipes are based on authentic ones and are delicious."

"What's saffron?" Dylan asked, his forehead creased as he contemplated the menu.

"It's like a spice. It colors things yellow orange," Anne answered. "The rice won't be white."

Dylan went back to studying the food offered, while Caleb set his menu down. "I think I'll have the beef with sesame-ginger glaze."

"Me, too," Dylan said, putting his menu down as well.

"Just to be different I'm trying the saffron rice with sausage, peppers and shrimp."

Dylan wrinkled his nose. "I don't think I would like yellow-orange rice. Rice is supposed to be white."

"It can be brown, too." Anne took a sip of her ice water, relishing its coolness as it slid down her throat.

"Yuck! Brown?" Dylan folded his arms over the menu on the table before he changed the subject. "I saw some kids dressed up in old-timey clothes. That looked cool."

"We'll come back and do that one day. There's a lot we didn't get to do at both places. And Yorktown is fun to visit." Caleb gathered up the menus for their server, who appeared at his side.

After their orders were taken, Dylan asked, "Come back?"

"Sure. I bought you both tickets that are good for the next year. I knew we wouldn't be able to do these places justice in just one day so I settled for whetting your appetite, so to speak. Would you like to come back?" Caleb looked from Dylan to Anne.

"Yes," Anne answered at the same time Dylan did.

They all laughed, the sound rivaling the music being sung for the guests by some balladeers. Anne settled back in her chair to enjoy a wonderful dinner to top off a wonderful day. A warmth suffused her at the prospects that a day like today wouldn't be a one-time deal. Caleb wanted to do it again with both Dylan and her—like a family.

Anne rushed toward the kitchen to grab something quick to eat before she headed for the church. She'd spent too long worrying over what to wear to baby-sit children in the nursery—this from a woman who never used to worry over what she wore anywhere. But over the past week she had bought some additions to her wardrobe that gave her choices beyond gray, black and navy blue.

She glanced down at her long denim jumper with red piping and several pockets—she figured she would need the pockets while working with young children—and her long-sleeved red cotton shirt. Had she gone overboard with color?

When Anne pushed open the kitchen door, her parents glanced up at her. A frown marred the perfection of her mother's carefully made-up face. An expression of equal displeasure graced her father.

"It's eight on Sunday morning. Where are you going so early? I thought we would talk and catch up before your father and I have to leave this afternoon for the next week."

Her mother's tone brought Anne up short. Standing on the other side of the table from her parents, she drew in a fortifying breath. "We've had the past few days. Why didn't you say anything then? I've committed myself to working in the nursery at the Chestnut Grove Community Church."

"You're going to church now? Is that because of that young man who was here the other night?" Her father folded the newspaper he had been reading and slapped it down on the table.

Anne pulled herself up straight, her shoulders back. "I'm helping in the nursery. And if you must know, I'm taking a good hard look at my life because of *that young man*." Her stomach churned with suppressed emotions she had kept locked up inside her for years.

"There's nothing wrong with your life." Her mother rose and went to the coffeepot to pour some more.

"How would you know? You two are

rarely here and when you are you hardly have anything to say to me. I might as well be invisible to you." The second she said what was really on her mind—what had been for a long time—she pressed her lips together to still any further outpouring. No matter what she told her parents, in the end they wouldn't understand or, she suspected, care.

"Anne, that's no way to talk to your mother."

Tears threatened to fill her eyes. Anne wouldn't let her parents see her cry. She'd shed many tears over the years because of their lack of love and support. She whirled around, saying, "I'm late. I hope you have a nice week."

Hurrying from the house, Anne didn't stop until she was seated behind the steering wheel and trying to compose herself enough to drive to the church. Her hands shook. Tears rolled down her face and fell onto her lap. She squeezed her eyes closed and inhaled shallow breaths. Lungs burning, she tried to breathe deeper, but with her chest constricting them, it was impossible.

She remembered the story in the Bible that Caleb had given her about the prodigal son. Would it take leaving her parents and returning years later to be loved by them?

She was afraid the answer was no and that broke her heart.

With her hands still quivering, she started the car and pulled out of the driveway. She needed to move to her own apartment even though she would have a hard time affording to live on her own. If she had to work two jobs she would, because living with her parents, even though they were rarely there, was undermining her flowering self-confidence, her developing new image of herself.

When Anne arrived at the church, the parking lot was beginning to fill with cars. She found a place near the rear door by the nursery. Even though she didn't attend the church, she had been inside it on a number of occasions, the last being Pilar and Rachel's double wedding.

She intended to slip into the church through the back door and avoid the people going in by the sanctuary, but Caleb saw her and waved. She halted her step and waited for him to join her.

"You look lovely and rested, Anne. I was afraid I had worn you out yesterday and you would pass on helping with the nursery."

"If I say I'm going to do something, I do. I did go right to bed when we got home last night from Williamsburg. I think I walked at least ten or fifteen miles yesterday. But I had a great time and, more importantly, Dylan did, too."

"Yes, he did. I hated waking him up on the ride home last night. I hated returning him to the Givens' house."

Anne laid her hand on his arm. It felt so natural to touch Caleb now. "You'll hear soon. I can't see the state turning you down."

"If I get to be a foster parent, I'll have to move to a bigger place. I only have a one bedroom right now."

"You know, I was thinking about moving this morning, too. I think it's time for me to have my own apartment. I'll have to find one that is reasonably priced, however."

"Mine is. You could have mine if I have to move."

The idea of living in the apartment that Caleb had occupied for so long sent her heart pounding against her rib cage. Her mouth felt as though she hadn't had a drink of water in days. She suddenly realized she wanted more from their relationship than friendship and wasn't sure how to control that need.

"I can show it to you and you can decide. I probably should start looking for a new place myself. That way I'll be prepared when the state gives its okay." Caleb started walking toward the front entrance.

"That's good. Positive thinking. I like it." Anne fell into step beside him, and saw the crowd gathered in the nave, many of them people she had known all her life.

Rachel waved to them. Pilar stopped her before she could escape down the hall to the nursery.

"I like the new look," Pilar said, nodding her head toward Caleb, who had been stopped by Jared and Meg Kierney. "Is he the reason for the change?"

"Actually I have to put the blame at Gina, Tiffany and Nikki's feet."

"The fall carnival?"

"Yep. They were bound and determined to make me over. I feel like I was on one of those makeover shows on TV. I expected a cameraman to reveal himself at any moment the whole time they were fussing over me."

"I like the haircut and I think you wearing it down about your face is great. Softens your look."

"It took some getting use to, but I like it, too." Anne patted her head, aware that Meg and Jared were staring at her. Finally the couple weaved their way through the crowd. Each carried one of their twins.

"I hear you're going to be in the nursery. Luke and Chance will like that." Meg shifted Chance to her other arm as he strained to get down. "Jared, we'd better get these two to the room."

Anne walked with Meg and Jared to the nursery. She was glad so many of her friends were at the church. She didn't feel so awkward.

Clothed in a vintage dress of pale blue from the sixties, Leah Paxson greeted the twins at the door with two large shirts that had dried paint on them. "We're going to be messy today."

"What do you have planned?" Meg asked, releasing her wiggling boy so Leah could slip the shirt over his head.

"Finger painting with pudding." Leah smiled at Anne. "I'm so glad you're gonna help me out. I can always use an extra pair of hands."

"Just tell me what to do and I'll do it." Anne stepped into the room, and Leah closed the bottom part of the door so the children couldn't get out.

"Oh, I like you already. Right now we're refereeing until all the children arrive, then I'll get the activities started. We'll finger paint first, then make a necklace out of Fruit

Loops." Leah stood, flipping her long, light brown hair behind her shoulders.

Anne never thought of herself as tall, but she was in comparison to Leah. Anne ended up sitting on the floor to play with several of the children while Leah checked the newcomers in. When church service started, Leah called for the children's attention, and to Anne's surprise most of them listened to her instructions. Anne helped her seat them at the two long tables, then Leah pulled out the large sheets of paper and the containers of pudding—chocolate, vanilla, strawberry.

"Strawberry pudding?" Anne wrinkled her nose.

"I added red food coloring to vanilla so we would have several different colors. I find the children enjoy the pudding better than finger paints. Little hands often end up in mouths and pudding tastes better." Leah squatted down next to Chance to help him get started.

"Where are the babies?" Anne counted ten children, all between two and four years of age.

"In another room with someone else. We have a third room for the older children."

"Do you usually do this by yourself?"

"No, I always have a helper, but she recently moved. Caleb helped one Sunday and another woman last week. I hope to have a regular assistant soon."

Anne bent over and removed a container of chocolate pudding from a little girl's hands who was hugging it to her chest and not sharing. The child stared up at her, her lower lip trembling as tears gathered in her big brown eyes. Anne put the container back in the middle of the table for the others to use, then knelt down next to the girl.

"What's your name?" Anne asked.

"Laurie," she said, drawing in raspy breaths as she fought her tears.

"How old are you?"

Sniffling, the girl held up three chubby fingers.

"Oh, my, you are a big girl."

Through the tears the child grinned. "Mama says I am, especially now that I have a little brother."

Anne leaned close and whispered into her ear, "This is my first day. Can I ask a favor of you?"

Laurie nodded several times.

"Will you help me make sure everyone at this table gets to use all the different kinds of puddings?"

She bobbed her head up and down.

Anne stood and watched as Laurie supervised the pudding use. The little girl looked up at Anne a few times as though checking to make sure she was doing a good job and that Anne was watching her. Anne gave her a thumbs-up sign, and the child beamed from ear to ear with two big dimples in her cheeks that reminded Anne of hers.

Leah sidestepped until she was next to Anne. "You're a natural. Laurie can be difficult. She's been upset because of her new baby brother and hasn't been sharing with the others the past few months."

"I would like to help you on a regular basis if you want."

"If I want? Are you kidding! I want." Leah grinned as wide as Laurie, her topaz colored eyes sparkling.

The rest of the time working in the nursery passed quickly. Before Anne realized it, the room was empty and Caleb waited at the door for her. Tired but happy, Anne gathered her purse, said goodbye to Leah and left.

Caleb walked with her down the long hallway toward the front of the church, his hand touching the small of her back. "I hope you'll come to the youth center this afternoon for our weekly meeting."

Anne had questions she wanted answered

from reading two of the gospels in the Bible. "Sure."

"Good. I thought we could grab something to eat afterwards."

She wanted to ask him if he was asking her out on a date. Their relationship was so unclear to her. Friends? Or, something more? But Anne didn't have the nerve to say the words out loud. "That sounds nice," she said instead, responding to the warmth of his smile.

Chapter Nine

Sunday evening after eating at the Starlight Diner, Caleb unlocked the door to his apartment and let Anne enter first. "What do you think?" He swept his arm across his body to indicate the small living room.

Anne surveyed the area, a navy blue couch along one wall with a coffee table in front of it and one tan leather lounge chair off to its side. Along another wall were three bookcases overflowing with all kinds of different books, from nonfiction to biographies to thrillers. Even though the apartment was neat, nothing out of place, Anne felt a warmth in the pictures and the knickknacks on the tables.

One intricately woven basket on the coffee table captured her attention. Its masterful geometric design prompted her to ask,

"Where did you get that?" Anne gestured toward the basket.

"In Africa."

"I didn't realize you've been to Africa."

"Right after I completed my master's degree in child psychology, I served the Lord for four years in Africa at a mission."

"Why did you come back to the States?"

"My mother needed me. She became very ill. I'd been home six months when she died."

"Why didn't you go back to Africa after that?"

"Because I'd discovered Chestnut Grove and the youth center. I couldn't leave the job. I'd been here three months when Mom passed away."

"You've been here how long?" Anne made a slow circle, checking out the small kitchenette with a table that seated two.

"A little over two years." Caleb crossed the room and opened one of two doors and stood back for her to look inside.

Anne stuck her head into the bedroom, noting again Caleb's neatness. The double bed was made with a navy blue bedspread. Other than a chest of drawers and one bedside table with a lamp, clock and Bible, there wasn't any more room for other pieces of furniture. "Where's the bathroom?"

Caleb stepped to the other door and opened it.

Anne inspected the tiny room with hardly any space to turn around in. No bathtub. Only a shower stall. That was okay. She rarely took baths. And the best part of the apartment was its rent. Very affordable. The elderly couple who lived below Caleb in the rest of the house were nice and friendly, too. "If you have to move, I would love to rent this apartment. Do you think the Morgans would approve of me?"

With his shoulder cushioned against the wall next to the bathroom door, Caleb said, "With my recommendation they will. I hate to leave them. They have been so good to me. But if I become a foster parent, I'll have to. As you can see," he indicated the area around him, "this place is small, only meant for one person."

"But great for me. I appreciate you showing me your apartment."

Caleb pushed himself away from the wall. "Then we'll wait and see what the state decides before approaching Neil and Bertha about the change." He walked toward the door. "I'd better get you home. Tomorrow is a work day."

Anne looked at the clock on his wall in the

kitchen area and saw that it was already nine. With Caleb, time flew by.

"Speaking of work, did you ever find anything in those ledgers you almost broke your neck trying to get down?"

She batted her eyelashes and said, "But my Prince Charming came to my rescue."

"You're just lucky I was there."

"If I remember correctly, it was because you were there that I fell in the first place. If you hadn't scared me, I would have been fine. I had everything under control."

He chuckled. "You don't know that for sure."

Anne led the way down the narrow flight of stairs at the side of the house. Earlier when they had first arrived, Caleb had told her that he had a key to the Morgans' front door, but after eight he didn't like to use it because they went to bed early. "In answer to your question I haven't found a thing in the old account books, which makes me wonder if there were *two* sets of books kept somewhere."

"I still have a hard time believing Barnaby Harcourt illegally adopted out children."

Anne walked beside Caleb toward his Suburban. "Yeah and poor Kelly is having to clean up his mess. The worse part is that the agency's reputation has suffered. We've done so much good over the years, and yet right now people are focusing on the wrong that Barnaby did, not the good."

Caleb reached around her and opened the passenger door. "That's human nature for you."

"And you should know, being a psychologist." Anne slid into the car.

"My specialty is children."

"There really isn't that much difference. It's just that our flaws aren't as ingrained when we're children."

Caleb came around the front of the Suburban and climbed in. "Children are more willing to change."

"Change is possible at any age."

"Only if we want it." Caleb switched on the car and pulled out of the driveway.

"Sure. But I'm finding myself changing. Two months ago I wouldn't have considered moving away from my parents. I have rarely gone against their wishes, and they won't be too happy with my decision when I tell them." She thought of that confrontation and a shudder jolted her. She would deal with that when the time came, she decided, pushing the worry to the background. "They see me as their caretaker since they are gone so much."

"What do you see yourself as?"

"Someone who's finally discovering who she is."

"Does God fit into that picture? I know you've been reading the Bible and asking questions at our meetings."

"Truthfully I'm not one hundred percent sure." She wanted to tell him, yes, she believed, but she couldn't. She knew how important that was to him, but she would always be one hundred percent truthful with Caleb.

He parked out in front of her house, the light from the street lamp illuminating his face, set in a thoughtful expression.

"I'll pick you up Wednesday evening to go to the hospital. Dinner afterwards?"

"Sure." The tension in the car swirled about her, making her very aware that she had disappointed Caleb. But no matter how much she cared—loved—him she wouldn't profess a belief in the Lord without really believing. That wasn't her nor was it something she was willing to fake in order to have Caleb's interest.

"I have something for you. Can you come in for a few minutes?"

His chest expanded in a deep breath. He released his knuckle-white grip on the steering wheel and opened the car door. She waited for him to come around and open her side as though he was courting her, which he wasn't, especially since his disappointment in her was so obvious.

Silence charged the short walk up to her house. Even the night sounds were quiet as Anne climbed the steps to the porch. Tension continued to hum between them like a machine used to drown out background noise.

In the house she motioned for him to follow her to the back room. When she flipped on the light, a soft glow flooded her work area.

"As you can see, this is where I paint. I wanted to show you."

Caleb stood back by the entrance and surveyed the room. An easel sat by the window that received the morning light. There was a table full of supplies, oils, brushes, a dirty cloth. As he took in what she was showing him, his throat and heart swelled with emotions that contradicted what he should feel after what she had disclosed in the car. She was letting him see a part of herself that others didn't. He felt gifted by her gesture and couldn't find the words to express the emotions bubbling in him.

"And I wanted to give you this." She strode to the corner and picked up a canvas, then came back to him.

He moved farther into the room and grasped the picture she thrust at him, her arms held stiffly, her hold on the frame tight. She released her death grip, and he took her gift, those feelings he couldn't control floating to the surface.

It was an oil painting of the youth center with him sitting on the front steps cradling a mug between his hands. His likeness was uncanny down to his expression of wonderment at the beauty before him. This was a picture of that first day she'd come to the center to help with the fall carnival. He was touched and honored by her gift, as though she had given a part of herself to him in that moment. And in a way she had.

"Thank you, Anne." The words barely came out of his mouth because his throat was swollen with feelings he was desperately trying to deny and couldn't.

He was falling in love with Anne, a non-Christian. He'd dedicated his whole life to Christ as his Savior. *How can I love someone who doesn't share my love of Jesus?* He gripped the painting to him, pain from the force of his grasp shooting up his arm.

"You're welcome. I've been working on this for several weeks. I wasn't sure what I was going to do with it, but I saw a blank place on your wall that could use a picture and I immediately thought of mine."

"But you don't let others see your paintings. If someone asks, I'll have to tell them who the artist is."

"I wouldn't expect anything less than the truth from you and that's okay if you tell them. I'm discovering it's important to acknowledge who you are. Painting is an important part of who I am and I'm not going to deny it any longer."

He grinned. "Then I'll gladly display this picture for all to see. People will be knocking on your door asking you to paint a portrait of them. Will you be ready for that?"

She laughed, heading out into the hallway. When he left her work room, she switched off the light and shut the door. "I won't worry about that."

"Why not?"

"I just paint for myself. I'm not an artist and I usually don't do portraits, mostly landscapes."

"If you paint, then you're an artist."

She remembered the first time she'd shown her parents one of her paintings when she'd been in high school, and had finally worked up the courage to subject her art for another to see. They'd looked at it for a few seconds, then given it back to her. The one comment her father had said as she'd left the kitchen was that she might think about not using so many colors next time. Not "good try." Nothing. After that, she hadn't let anyone see her work until recently.

Walking toward the entry hall, Anne asked, "So with that assumption, if I write, then I'm an author?"

His chuckles danced down her spine. "Yes, I like that."

"Since most people write in their everyday life, there are an awfully lot of authors out there."

"Most poor and struggling."

"The starving artist."

"Exactly." He faced her and clasped her hands. "Which brings me to a favor I want to ask you."

His touch caused her breath to catch in her throat, and she would have done anything in that moment. "What?"

"I'm giving the sermon next week and I was hoping you would come hear me either at the early or late service."

"What are you speaking on?"

"I haven't decided yet so it will be a surprise."

"So long as it isn't a surprise to you."

He laughed—a deep, robust sound that permeated the small entry hall. "I have in the past done some speeches off the top of my head, but not often. I like to have notes to work off of."

"I would need the whole speech written out word for word and a screen to hide behind before I would even consider getting up in front of people. And even then I don't think I could do it. I'm sure my legs and voice would give out."

"Before or after you got up there to speak?"

"I don't know and I don't ever intend to find out. I'm a behind-the-scenes kind of person, and I don't think that will ever change about me."

"And I'm the kind of person who likes to stand in the middle of the stage, so to speak."

"We are very different."

Caleb inched forward until little space was between them. "I don't know that we're that different. We both love children. We're both artists of sorts—you with your painting and me with my writing, sermons and articles." He released one hand and raked it through her hair until he cupped the back of her head. "And I hope I am as caring and warm as you are."

His last sentence was spoken on a faint whisper as he lowered his mouth toward hers. It felt as though her heart stopped beating, then began to crash against her rib cage in a quick cadence that made her light-headed. The world spun out of control as his lips feathered across hers, ever so softly, teasing her.

Then he wound his arms around her and brought her against him, his mouth taking possession of hers in a deep kiss that rocked her to her soul and robbed her of coherent thought. When he pulled back, she experienced bereavement as if she had lost something precious and dear to her heart.

He stepped away until there were several feet between them. "I shouldn't have kissed you, but I don't regret one second of that kiss, Anne."

Neither did she. She would treasure it forever. Her throat tight, she swallowed hard, trying to find the words to describe how she felt. There was none that would do justice to the emotions she experienced while in his embrace.

His eyes gleaming with a smile, he backed up, never taking his gaze from her face. "If I don't see you before Wednesday, I'll pick you up at Tiny Blessings at five." He turned to open the door, stopped and glanced at her. "You never told me if you would come hear me give a sermon next Sunday."

"Yes," she murmured. "I'm looking forward to hearing you speak." And she meant it. When he spoke of Jesus, he made Him come alive. Caleb gave her hope and a sense that someone cared—not just Caleb, but God. Was it possible?

The first work day of the week was glorious, Anne thought as she left Tiny Blessings with her sack lunch and strolled toward Winchester Park, where she planned to spend an hour eating her sandwich and enjoying the beauty of a fall day. A hint of crispness laced the breeze that teased the strands of her hair. The sun beat down on her and alleviated any coolness.

In the park she chose a bench near Main Street that afforded her a view of the downtown and the small man-made pond. Nearby she saw the playground with young children playing and their mothers watching. With a heavy sigh, she unwrapped her tuna fish sandwich and took a bite, wishing she was one of those young mothers watching her child.

She should be tired, having slept little the

night before. All she'd been able to think about was Caleb and his kiss. Even if their relationship didn't go beyond that one kiss, she would cherish it and the feelings that had washed over her.

Her lips tingled. Putting her sandwich on the foil in her lap, she brushed her fingertips across her mouth, reliving the kiss that gave her hope one day she might be a mother to a horde of children and sitting at the playground watching them enjoy a beautiful autumn day.

Another sigh escaped between her lips. She finished her sandwich and apple, then crushed the sack and foil into a ball and tossed it in the trash can beside the bench. Lingering for a few more minutes, she inhaled the earthy scent of freshly mowed grass mingling with the aroma of grilled meat coming from the Starlight Diner.

With a glance toward the restaurant, Anne straightened, her hands clenching the edge of the wooden seat. Caleb exited the diner with a woman whom Anne had never seen before, a tall gorgeous woman with very long dark hair, the breeze sending strands dancing about her face. He laughed at something she said, his hand placed casually at the small of her back as they started down the street toward the youth center.

Anne's stomach plummeted, as though she had been thrown off a skyscraper and was falling. Glued to the bench, she watched them walk away until they disappeared from view. Then every rigid muscle in her body seemed to liquify at the same time. She sank against the wooden slats, fighting the urge to cry.

She had never been jealous of another woman because she had never allowed herself to care about a man enough to be jealous of any rival. But in that brief glimpse of Caleb with the stranger, Anne had experienced envy and didn't like it. Last night she had been on top of the world. Today she had hit rock bottom.

Caleb opened the door to the youth center and let Kimberly Forrester enter first. "I'll give you the grand tour. A lot has been done to this building since I took over."

"In your last e-mail you said the fall carnival was a success."

"We'll be able to get all the new rec equipment we've needed for a while and fund an expansion of the after-school program I've wanted to do for some time."

"That's nice." Kimberly peered into the arts-and-crafts room and the gym. When she looked into the TV room, she said, "You'll be needing a new couch and some chairs soon."

"Yeah, that's next on my list. The kids really use that room not just to watch television but as a meeting room." Caleb gestured toward his office. "Let's go in here to talk."

Kimberly sat in a padded chair in front of a large window, while Caleb took the seat across from her. A small round table separated them.

"You really enjoy working with kids." Kimberly crossed her legs and relaxed back.

"You know that's always been my vision of my future."

"Yes. I can still remember when we met in Africa my first day at the mission. You were refereeing a soccer game with some kids who were getting a little carried away."

Caleb laughed, thinking back to that day. "You mean *I* got carried away, literally. I ended up in the clinic at the mission and had to get four stitches."

"But we met because of that mishap on the field."

"Yeah, when I got in the way of a determined teen trying to do a header into the goal." Caleb put his elbows on his thighs and loosely clasped his hands between his legs.

"Why didn't you tell me you were coming back to the States?"

She smiled, her green eyes, tilted up slightly at the corners, lighting up. "Because I wanted to surprise you."

"Well, you have. When you showed up in the hallway out there this morning, I thought I was dreaming."

"I'm glad you said dreaming instead of having a nightmare."

He chuckled. "Never, Kimberly. We've been friends for a long time."

Her expression grew serious. "Just friends? Right before you returned to the States, we were talking of taking our relationship to the next level. Remember our discussions about serving in a mission together in a more remote area than we were already in Africa?"

"Yes." That seemed a long time ago, he thought. So much has happened between then and now. A picture of Anne popped into his mind.

"My ministry organization wants me to start a mission farther up the river in a pretty isolated part of the jungle. They asked me to put a team of three more people together. My first thought was of you. There's so much to do in that part of Africa. We would be reaching out to people who haven't heard a lot about Jesus."

Another dream come true, Caleb acknowledged, but again Anne crept into his thoughts, an image of her smiling at him with a dazed look on her face after he had kissed her. He shouldn't have kissed her, but he couldn't help himself when he'd received that painting from her and he'd realized the importance of the gift.

"Caleb, come back to Africa with me as my husband. I want to start this mission with you by my side. There will be a lot of children to reach out to at the new mission, ones who do not know about Christ. I can't think of anyone else I want to spend my life with. We believe in the same things. We have the same goals and outlook on life. That's a great basis for a marriage and hopefully one day a family."

Kimberly's words rekindled dreams they had talked about while working together in Africa, before he'd had to return to the United States and had gotten caught up in the youth center. He really cared for Kimberly and loved her as a good friend. They believed in the same thing—the Lord as their Heavenly Father. Was that enough to base a marriage on? Could he marry Kimberly knowing his heart lay with Anne?

Caleb rose. "I don't know if I can walk away from this center and the kids here."

"Anyone can do this, Caleb. Not everyone can be a missionary in a remote part of Africa. You can. We can really make a difference over there. We can reach people who haven't been graced with the Good News, who don't have much in their lives and struggle each day just to make it to the next one."

Her ardent words touched a deep-seated need in him, but he couldn't ignore what needed to be done here in Chestnut Grove, either. And he wasn't so sure just anyone could step into his job and do what had to be done. "I wish the decision was as easy as you make it sound. It's something I have to pray about. Going to Africa again is a big step, but marriage is even a bigger one to me."

Kimberly came to her feet. "We would have a good marriage based on mutual friendship, respect and a belief in Christ. From what I've seen, that is a better basis for a marriage than what most people base one on."

But what about passion and love, Caleb thought, remembering the deep love his parents had had for each other. He wanted that. "Give me some time."

"I'm returning to Africa in two weeks. I'm

staying with my parents in Fairfax. I hope you'll drive up and come to dinner some evening." Kimberly started for the door.

"I'll call soon. We'll talk some more and I want you to come speak to my kids before you go back to Africa. I want you to tell them about Africa and your work."

"I wish I could meet them this afternoon, but I've got that appointment with the church leaders in an hour in Richmond about the funding."

On the steps of the center Caleb hugged Kimberly and kissed her on the cheek. "Good luck with your meeting."

At her car Kimberly waved goodbye and Caleb returned the gesture. He watched her drive away, a feeling of dread cloaking him. He had a decision he needed to make that he didn't want to. What Kimberly offered was very enticing. But he also had to consider the kids in Chestnut Grove, the center he had started and built from almost nothing. Then there was Dylan, who was desperately searching for a home and someone to love him unconditionally. He couldn't be his foster parent from Africa.

And he needed to consider Anne. What if she never believed in Jesus? Could he stay in Chestnut Grove and be around her and want her when he knew there could be no real future for them as a couple? Each time he would see her he would die a little inside. The feelings he was experiencing with her weren't going to go away simply because he wished them to. Distance might be the only way for him to keep his sanity.

So much to think about. *God, what do I do? Help me! I want it all—a wife, a family, to serve You and a purpose in life.* The weight of his decision bore down on him, making his steps back into the youth center leaden.

Chapter Ten

"You've been awfully quiet tonight. Are you okay?" Caleb asked as he drove into the outskirts of Chestnut Grove.

"I'm fine. Just tired. Today was a long one." Anne massaged her temples.

At the hospital Caleb remembered the knitted forehead, her lips firmed into a straight line, not exactly a frown but not her usual serene smile when she held the babies. Something was wrong. He didn't need a Mack truck to run over him to figure that one out. "Are you getting a migraine?"

She shook her head.

Had she heard about Kimberly being back in the States? A dozen times tonight he had tried to bring up the subject of Kimberly's visit and her offer. He hadn't found the words to explain to Anne because confusion reigned inside him. What Kimberly had offered was enticing and if he had stayed in Africa, he wondered where their relationship would have gone. But he hadn't stayed and he'd met Anne. Could he give his heart totally to a woman who didn't believe in God, especially with his life's work being the spreading of the Good News? He didn't know what to think or feel and so far his prayers hadn't been answered. He didn't have a solution to his dilemma.

"I need to grab something at the center. Do you mind if we stop by there before I take you home?" Caleb asked, realizing he wanted to work on the order for the rec equipment. He didn't think he would be sleeping tonight. He certainly hadn't slept well the past two nights since Kimberly's proposal.

"Sure," she replied absently, her head turned so she was staring out the side window as they drove down Main Street.

At the center Anne came with him into the building. He headed straight for his office a few steps ahead of her.

When she entered the room, he pivoted toward her and said, "I think we need to talk."

"When someone says that it usually doesn't bode well."

Caleb moved to the group of chairs and

sat, waiting for Anne to do likewise. She perched on the edge of the chair as though any minute she would take flight and leave him.

She gripped the seat, tension locking her arms. "What did you need to talk about?"

"I've been offered a job. In Africa." Beads of sweat popped out on his forehead. This wasn't easy and he wasn't doing a good job. "Actually, it's more than that. A good friend, Kimberly Forrester, is here in the States from Africa. We used to work together at a mission over there. We'd always talked about opening a mission farther up the river in a more remote part of the jungle and she has finally gotten funding to do that. She wants me to be a part of that—as her husband."

Anne stopped breathing for a few seconds. Then suddenly her heart began to hammer against her rib cage and her blood pounded in her ears. So that was who he had been with on Monday. It was even worse than she had thought. "What are you planning to do?"

"I don't know." He clasped his hands together, nothing casual about him. "I have to ask myself if this is what God wants me to do. I won't kid you—there's a part of me that wants to go back to Africa. I felt as though I'd done a lot of good there."

"You've done a lot of good here, too."

"Have I? Sometimes I wonder."

"What about Dylan?"

Caleb's shoulders sagged forward. "You're the one who reached him. I just came along for the ride."

"But you've applied to be his foster parent."

"I know. But maybe Dylan would be better off with someone like the Frasers. They'll be able to take in a new foster child soon. Dylan needs both a mother and father. Seeing him with you tells me that."

Upset and not sure what to do, Anne surged to her feet, staring down at him. "I—I—" Her words froze in her throat. Caleb had given her a glimpse of what it could be like, cherished by a man, and he was going to leave her. How could she fight that? How could she fight God for him?

He gripped the arms of the chair and shoved himself upward, his face set in a deep frown that made his eyes a dark blue like a sky right before a storm. "I haven't done a very good job of explaining my dilemma, Anne. My feelings."

He was too close. She wanted to touch him, hold him. Stepping back, she said, "What are your feelings?"

Plunging his hands through his hair, his jaw clenched, he shook his head. "Conflicting ones."

Another step back. "From my perspective you have a choice between staying here and running the youth center and possibly becoming Dylan's foster parent or going to Africa, setting up a new mission and marrying Kimberly. Isn't that it?"

He laughed, but there was no humor in the sound. "I wish it were that simple. You forgot to mention you in all the choices."

One more step and she was flattened against the closed door to his office. She fumbled for the handle and grasped it so tight that pain streaked up her arm. "I'm not sure that I'm involved in your decision."

Again he laughed, a grating sound that screeched down her spine. "You are very much involved in my decision for my future."

"I am?" Her grip slackened and her arm fell to her side.

"I'm falling in love with you but—" He looked away for a long moment, clearing his throat. "Do you believe in God, Anne?"

Everything she wanted was in her grasp if she lied to him and told him yes. Staring into his endearing features, she couldn't do that.

His faith was so important to him and she wouldn't lie about hers. "I don't know, Caleb. I've been reading the gospels and I can remember my times in church with Grandma Rose, but I don't have a ready answer for you yet. I wish I did because I'm falling in love with you and I want to make you happy."

He moved closer until she could lay her hand over his heart if she chose to. "You love me?"

Tears filled her eyes at the amazement in his expression. She nodded, unable to say anything.

"Do you think you'll ever believe in our Lord?" Hope shone in his eyes, making them light blue.

"I can't answer that. It isn't a simple question." She didn't know if she could turn control of her life over to the Lord. She'd have such little control in her life that what little she possessed she didn't want to let go of—even for Caleb's God.

The hope blossoming in his expression evaporated. "I was engaged to a woman who I thought would come around to believing in Jesus. We were two weeks from walking down the aisle when she confessed to me she didn't truly believe and didn't see that changing in her future. She wanted me to go into private practice as a child psychologist and make a lot of money. I didn't see the future as she did. We broke up but the hurt cut deep. I thought I could convert her to Christianity. She let me think I could because she wanted to get married. I won't go through that again. I only want to marry one time."

"I agree a marriage must be based on love, mutual respect and fundamental beliefs. I only want to marry one time, too."

"Then you see my dilemma."

"Yes." She grasped the handle, yanked open the door and headed for the parking lot.

She was changing, evolving into a different person, but could that person accept Christ into her life and blindly follow Him? For so many years she hadn't stood up for herself, had even hidden from life. Now she was finding there was a lot about herself that she could celebrate. It had felt good to make the decision to move out from her parents' house, to show another person her paintings.

Caleb exited the building a few minutes after her, his pace slow as though he were contemplating something. Anne watched him stride toward her. Her heart cracked at the sight of his expression in the streetlight. He'd erected a barrier between them, as if he were starting to distance himself from her in order to protect himself. She saw the signs because she had done that to others all her life.

But she didn't want to lose his friendship, too. It was that friendship that had given her the emotional strength to take the necessary steps to change.

When he slid into the driver's seat and started the engine, Anne began to say something, took another look at his hard features, his mouth firmed in a straight line, his hands clutching the cold plastic of the steering wheel. Instead, she shivered, a chill flowing from him to her.

Don't shut me out. Anne wanted to shout those words, but she was afraid he wouldn't really hear them, that he'd already shut his mind to her.

When Caleb turned onto Anne's street, he noticed Zach's car in her driveway. "Are you expecting Zach?"

Alert, Anne straightened. "No. Why would he be here unless," she paused, "unless something's wrong? Maybe something's happened to Pilar."

Caleb parked in front of Anne's house, and before he had his door open, she was out of his Suburban and running up the steps toward Zach, who stood on the porch. Caleb hurried after her. Worry took hold and grew when he saw the serious expression on his friend's face.

"Is something wrong with Pilar?" Anne asked before Zach could say anything.

"No, she's fine. I'm here because Dylan is gone again, but this time I think his father took him. Rex Givens called the police a few hours ago."

"He kidnapped Dylan?"

"I think Dylan called his father and asked him to pick him up. At least that is what Dylan's friends are saying. What I need from both of you is any place Dylan might have gone with his father. I know you've gotten pretty close with the boy so I thought he might have said something to either one of you." Zach loosened his tie. "We've checked out his father's apartment and the place where he's currently working. Nothing. We have an APB out on the car he's driving. Other than that, I've run out of ideas."

Caleb placed his hands on Anne's shoulders and felt her shudders. He squeezed, hoping to convey his support. "Other than the youth center I don't have the vaguest idea where he would go and certainly not with his father."

"Anne?" Zach asked.

"I don't, either. Are you sure he's with his father?"

"Not one hundred percent, but no one has seen Rob Taylor today."

"So there's a chance Dylan went off by himself again," Anne said, relief in her voice. "Have you checked the center?"

"No, but we can."

"Let Caleb and I do that. We were there a few minutes ago and didn't see him, but we only went into Caleb's office. If he's there, we'll call you immediately."

Zach hesitated.

"Please, Zach. I need to do something to help find Dylan."

Her plea ripped at Caleb's heart. He wanted to find Dylan, too, but there was a desperation in Anne that went beyond his feelings. She had connected with the boy on a level he hadn't.

"Fine."

Anne had already pivoted and was descending the steps when Zach answered. Caleb started after her, glanced back at his friend and asked, "You're pretty sure he's with his father?"

"Yep. A neighbor saw his car a few houses down from the Givens' earlier today."

"We'll check the center anyway. Maybe Dylan saw his father, then ran away again."

"Look, Caleb, at the moment I don't have anything better."

Anne was already in the car, drumming her fingers against her leg, when he climbed in. Caleb could feel her impatience as though it were a palpable force swirling around in the car.

"We'll find him," Caleb said to reassure her, but also himself. If Dylan's father had him, no telling where he was by now. In the three or four hours he had been missing they could be in another state. They could—

"I have a bad feeling about this."

Anne's tight voice sliced into his thoughts, producing his own bad feeling that had been festering deep in his heart.

On the drive back to the youth center, Anne stared at the scenery going by, not really seeing anything. Her mind could only think one thing: Dylan alone with his father again. *Please, Lord, lead us to Dylan. Help us find him before his father hurts him.*

For a second, surprise seized her. She didn't pray, hadn't really since visiting her grandmother years ago. But if it would help, she would do anything to get Dylan back safely.

When Caleb pulled into the parking lot at the center, Anne shoved open the door and hurried toward the building before he had turned off the engine. Her foot tapped impatiently as she waited for him to ascend the steps to the front door and unlock it.

Inside Anne threw on the lights as she moved through the rooms, calling out Dylan's name. Silence ruled. Caleb took one side of the hallway while she checked the rooms across from him. When she flipped on the light in the TV room, she expected to find Dylan curled up on the couch asleep. No Dylan. Disappointment and frustration wound about her in a vise-like grip.

At the end of the hall in the gym, sometimes cafeteria, both she and Caleb inspected every nook and cranny, even some places that it would be impossible for a child Dylan's size to fit. But this was the last room and Dylan wasn't at the center. Anne felt Caleb's desperation heightening and mirroring her own.

Standing in the middle of the gym, sober and fearful, Anne said, "He isn't here. His dad has him."

"I think so."

"No!" Tears swelled into her eyes and fell down her cheeks. "Please pray to your God and make it not so. His father used to beat Dylan, especially when he was drinking. He can't be with that man."

Caleb crossed the few feet separating them

and grasped Anne's hands. "Praying is a good thing to do. Pray with me, Anne."

With tears still streaming down her face, she nodded.

Caleb bowed his head. "Dear Heavenly Father, please protect Dylan and bring him home to us safe and sound. Help us to reach him. Amen."

"Amen," Anne mumbled, lifting her head and capturing his gaze. "It's got to work."

"God will take care of Dylan. God didn't bring him into our lives without a reason."

Through her glistening eyes she looked at him. "I wish I had your strong faith." Then maybe her heart wouldn't feel as if it were breaking into pieces.

"Come on. Let's fix some coffee and call Zach. We can stay here for a while and have Zach call us if they find out anything about Dylan." Caleb rubbed his thumbs across her cheeks, wiping away the traces of her tears.

"Coffee? Do you have any tea?"

He chuckled. "I think I can find a bag or two for you." He pulled her toward the kitchen off the gym.

Hugging a throw pillow to her chest, Anne lay curled on the old couch in the TV room, her long eyelashes fanning the tops of her pale cheeks as she slept. Caleb didn't have the heart to wake her up, and yet they probably needed to leave the youth center and try to get some rest in their own beds.

With a glance at his watch, he noted the late hour and sighed heavily. Midnight. Was Dylan someplace safe? Was he alone or with his father? Caleb wasn't sure which he preferred. Neither one was a good choice. He just wanted Dylan home with him.

Anne stirred, bringing her arm up to cover her eyes.

Caleb pushed himself out of his chair and stooped to shake her awake. "We need to leave, Anne."

Groaning, she brought her arm down and stared up at him. "Leave? Do we have to?" Sleep clung to each of her words.

"Afraid so."

"Did Zach call?" She swung her legs to the floor and sat up, hope brightening her features.

Caleb shook his head. "I would have wakened you if he had."

"A woman can wish."

"Yep, you can." He rose and offered her his hand.

She laid hers in his and let him pull her to her feet. "If Zach calls you, promise me you'll call right away, no matter what time it is."

"I wouldn't have it any other way, Anne." Caleb flipped the light switch as they left the room.

After he locked the front door to the youth center, he took Anne's hand and headed for his Suburban. His cell phone rang halfway to the car. Anne came up short and waited while Caleb answered.

"Caleb, it's Zach. We found Dylan. He's on the way to the hospital."

"Hospital? What happened?" Caleb gripped the phone until it hurt his hand.

"His father was driving and drinking and had an accident. Rob is perfectly fine. In fact, he walked away from the car wreck with only a few cuts and bruises. But Dylan's in serious condition. He's being transported to the Bon Secours Richmond Community Hospital."

"We're on our way. Thanks for letting us know."

Anne's face had gone white, looking eerie in the glow of the streetlight. "He's hurt?"

"There's been an accident. He's being taken to a hospital in Richmond."

"Why, Caleb? Dylan doesn't deserve any more problems. He's had too many in his short life."

"He has us now. We'll help him."

As he drove toward the hospital, Anne remained silent, her hands folded in her lap, her gaze trained straight ahead. Caleb started to say something, then decided to wait until they arrived and discovered how extensive Dylan's injuries were.

Lord, please be with Dylan. Protect him and watch over him. The whole way to the hospital, Caleb repeated that simple prayer.

Caleb found a parking space near the emergency room entrance, and with Anne, hurried inside. He started for the nurses' station when he saw Rex Givens sitting in the waiting room, slumped in the chair, his eyes closed as though he was asleep. Caleb headed into the room with Anne by his side, a pinched look about her mouth, her features still pale.

"Rex," Caleb said, shaking the man's shoulder.

Rex's eyes snapped open, and he sat up straight, dragging his hands down his face.

"Where's Dylan? How is he?"

"I got here about twenty minutes ago. The doctor is still working on him. The nurse said to wait here, and someone would be in to tell me what's going on." He covered a yawn with his hand, then knuckled his eyes. "I was sound asleep when Zach called. I guess I fell asleep again."

Anne stiffened. Caleb could feel her tension flowing off her in waves. He perched in the chair beside Rex while Anne sat next to him, so rigid that he was afraid she would break. Her silence worried Caleb.

A man with a white coat on and a stethoscope slung around his neck came into the room. He saw Caleb and asked, "Are you Mr. Givens?"

Caleb shook his head and jerked his thumb toward Rex.

Rex pushed himself to his feet as the doctor shortened the space between. "How's Dylan?"

Anne rose at the same time Caleb did. He sought her hand to hold, hoping to convey his support.

"I'm Dr. Winters, the surgeon called in to examine Dylan. I need to operate immediately. He's got some internal injuries. I'm not certain of the extent until I open him up. He also has a concussion and lacerations from hitting his head on the windshield, and a broken leg."

Anne's face paled even more. She gripped Caleb's hand tighter and leaned against him. "Is he going to make it?"

"He's in serious condition. I suspect his

spleen is ruptured. He's bleeding internally and I have to stop that. His right lung is punctured by a broken rib so I'll put in a chest tube. They're taking him to the OR right now. If you want to wait up there, I'll let you know when the operation is over. I'll know more about his chances then. Mr. Givens, the nurse has some papers for you to sign. Come this way."

Anne collapsed against Caleb. Caleb put his arm around her shoulders and supported her as her legs gave out.

As the doctor left the waiting room, Rex said, "I need to call Cora, too, and update her. I'll meet you upstairs in the waiting room."

For a long moment Caleb listened to the sounds of the hospital around him while he tried to digest all the information the doctor had given them. What if Dylan didn't make it? From the list of injuries it was a possibility. Fear gripped him as hard as Anne had.

"He could die, Caleb," Anne said, pushing away from him and facing him.

"No, he isn't going to. He will make it." *He had to,* Caleb silently added. God would protect Dylan. "I'd like to find the chapel and pray before going up to the waiting room. Will you come with me?" He held his breath while waiting for Anne's answer.

Finally, she nodded.

* * *

Anne couldn't sit another moment. Hours had passed since Dylan had been taken into the OR. Restless, she paced the length of the waiting room, thankful there was only Rex, Caleb and a young man waiting for news on his own loved one in the area. Inside she felt as though she were coming apart. Dylan didn't deserve this after all that had happened to him in his eleven short years.

Maybe their prayers would be answered. She hoped so. All she wanted to do was hold Dylan and give him the love he needed.

Glancing at Caleb, she marveled at how composed he was while her hands quivered and her stomach seethed. He had confidence that God would watch over Dylan. She wished her budding faith was that strong.

Dr. Winters, dressed in scrubs, appeared in the doorway. Everyone's attention shifted to him.

"Mr. Givens."

Rex stood. "Yes."

Dr. Winters approached Rex. "The surgery went well. We removed his spleen and put in a chest tube."

"So he'll be all right?" Anne asked, coming over to the doctor and Rex.

"The more serious problem isn't those injuries. We're concerned about his skull fracture. He's unconscious and will be watched closely in ICU."

"Can we see him?" Caleb came up behind Anne and clasped her shoulders.

"In a while."

Anne turned toward Caleb. "It doesn't sound good." She went into his embrace, seeking his warmth because she felt so cold, deep into the marrow of her bones.

"I've called Reverend Fraser and let him know what's going on. There are a whole lot of people praying for Dylan."

"What if that's not enough?"

Caleb ran his hand up and down her back. "Right now that's all we can do. Don't underestimate the power of prayer, Anne. It can work wonders."

"I hope so, Caleb. I hope so."

Every time Anne saw Dylan lying in the hospital bed, hooked up to a ventilator to breathe for him, her heart wrenched and tears jammed her throat. She wanted to cry, and yet she couldn't even release her tears. He looked lost, his face cut, his right leg in a cast, his mind and body deep in a coma.

"The doctor doesn't think he'll make it," Anne whispered to Caleb, her voice raw with emotions. "They basically have shut down his body in hopes that it will repair itself. What if it doesn't?" She spun about and found sanctuary in Caleb's arms for about five seconds until she remembered they were standing in ICU with Dylan a few feet away, having never regained consciousness after the car wreck, fighting for his life.

"Shh, Anne. He'll make it."

Suddenly the confidence in Caleb's voice didn't soothe. Anger bubbled to the surface. She pulled away as the nurse came to check on Dylan.

Moving out into the waiting area, Anne couldn't keep her anger at bay. It festered, burning a hole into her heart. "Why isn't he getting better? It's been three days. Nothing. What good are prayers when your God doesn't listen? Why would He take a boy like Dylan, who has gone through so much? What kind of God is He?"

Caleb scanned the people waiting, tugged Anne out into the hall, and said, "God works in His own time. We have to put our trust in the Lord that He knows what is best for everyone involved. I can't begin to second guess what His plan is, but He has one." He reached for her hand.

She stepped away, her back pressed up

against the wall. "There's nothing I can do to help Dylan. Why can't I help him?"

"You can. You can pray."

She clenched her teeth, balling her hands at her sides. "What good is that?"

Disappointment marked his features. Her anger grew. "I can't be who you want." She shoved past Caleb and almost ran toward the elevator. She had to get out of the hospital before she fell apart.

Caleb watched Anne hurrying to the elevator and slamming her palm against the down button. Sadness enveloped him, causing the beat of his heart to slow to a painful throb. Until just now he hadn't realized how much he had hoped that Anne would come to believe in God as he did, that they might have a future together. But that wasn't going to happen. He needed to make plans for himself that didn't include Anne. Rubbing his chest, he dragged deep breaths into his lungs, but nothing he did made the pain go away. He'd lost something precious today.

Her vision blurry, Anne fled the hospital with no idea where she was going. Outside, a cold dreary evening greeted her, mirroring the way she felt. Hugging her arms to her, she found a place near the entrance out of the way of the wind blowing and began pacing, trying to work off her anger. She shouldn't have said those things to Caleb. She had shocked and disappointed him—again. But lack of sleep and deep concern for Dylan had pushed her over the edge.

If only she could do something for Dylan.

Pray, Anne, an inner voice commanded.

But she had and it hadn't helped.

Have you really? Or did you just go through the motions? Did you really believe and put your whole heart into it?

Doubts plagued Anne. She would do anything to help Dylan, even pray to a god she wasn't sure existed.

Then she remembered her Grandma Rose's words. "Talking to God is like talking to a friend."

Is it that simple?

Anne paused in her pacing and looked up at the darkening sky as night fell. *God, if You can hear me, please don't let Dylan die. Give me a chance to love him as a little boy should be loved. He's had enough pain in his life. Please, God.* The words came haltingly into her mind, but they were from her heart.

"I feel like I can do this drive in my sleep," Caleb said as he drew closer to Chestnut Grove.

"Sleep? What is that?" Anne forced a light

tone into her voice, but the strain between them had been there ever since she had questioned him about God.

"It's only nine o'clock. The Starlight Diner is still open. Do you want to grab something to eat before I take you home? I know I don't have anything to eat in my apartment. If I'm not at work, I've been at the hospital."

"Same here. There's been no time to shop for groceries. And I have to admit I'm hungry. I haven't eaten all day and it's finally catching up with me."

Ten minutes later Caleb parked in front of the diner. Anne climbed from the car without waiting for him to open the door. The ride back from Richmond had only confirmed in her mind that they had become polite acquaintances again—any friendship they'd shared was forgotten.

Inside the diner Anne spied Pilar and Zach at a booth and strode toward them. Her friend and her new husband were sharing a slice of pecan pie.

Pilar looked up at her when she appeared. "Have a seat before you drop in your tracks, Anne."

Anne motioned behind her. "Caleb's with me."

"You both can join us. We're just finishing up dinner."

Because Anne suddenly didn't have the emotional strength to be alone with Caleb, she slipped into the booth across from Zach and Pilar. "I think I'll take you up on that offer. I have to say I'm tired."

"Well, I can certainly understand why." Pilar sipped her coffee. "When you aren't working, you're at the hospital. How's Dylan doing? Any news yet."

Anne shook her head while Caleb slid into the booth beside her. "He hasn't regained consciousness. He may stay in a coma for—" She couldn't voice aloud the possibility that Dylan might never wake up. Her mind reeled with emotions she didn't want to release, or she would find herself sobbing in front of her friends.

"Something good has come out of all of this," Zach said, finishing the last bite of pie.

Anne stiffened, curling her hands on the table into fists. "How can you say that?"

Chapter Eleven

"Because Rob Taylor has decided to give Dylan up for adoption. This latest incident has made it clear to the man he isn't good for Dylan and that his son would be better off with someone else." Zach covered Pilar's hand on the table. "He actually felt remorse for what he had done to his son."

"Good," Caleb said, opening his menu. "Dylan needs stability in his life and this will give him a chance to have it."

"If he comes out of his coma." Anne stared down at the menu and suddenly she didn't feel like eating anymore. All she could see in her mind's eye was Dylan lying in a hospital bed, his face cut up and bandaged, his leg in a cast and his eyes that remained closed. And the child's father walked away from the wreck with a few bruises. How was that fair? Anger and exhaustion tangled to weigh her down.

Zach swallowed the last of his coffee. "We need to go. Keep me posted about Dylan. We will both continue our prayers."

After Pilar and Zach left, Sandra came over and took their orders. Anne could only bring herself to get a house salad and a hot cup of tea. Her stomach knotted with tension, and she wasn't even sure she would be able to eat the salad.

Caleb scooted around to the other side to face her. "I'm worried about you, Anne. Gina even said something to me after she visited Dylan in the hospital."

"Because I'm upset about Dylan?"

"Yes. Let the anger go. It won't do you or Dylan any good. You aren't eating. You aren't sleeping."

"Forgive and forget?"

"To forgive, yes. To forget, no. We learn from the past so I think it's important to remember."

"Ah, like your experience with your ex-fiancée?"

His eyes darkened. "Yes."

At that moment Sandra brought them their salads and drinks. "I'll have your sandwich out in a few minutes, Caleb. How's Dylan doing?"

"No change. Still in a coma."

"I'll say an extra prayer for him."

"Thanks. He could use that. Will I see you tomorrow at church?"

"Of course." Sandra scurried back behind the counter.

"How about you, Anne? Will I see you tomorrow at church? I'm giving the sermon you said you would come to hear."

So much had happened since she had told him she would come to listen to his sermon. "I'll try to. I'm helping out in the nursery. I've volunteered to assist Leah at the early service and through Sunday school class."

"I'm glad. You're good with children."

Caleb searched the faces of the congregation sitting in the pews. Anne wasn't among them and disappointment took hold. He tried to come up with a reason she wouldn't be here to listen to his sermon. She could have been kept taking care of the children. She could—

He had to face the truth. Anne wasn't going to see the Lord as he did. They were going to remain poles apart on the issue of religion. And even if she came, it didn't really mean anything except that she was keeping her word to him to hear him speak. She'd told him she didn't know if she believed in God. What more did he need to help him make his decision?

Again Caleb looked out over the crowd in the sanctuary. Still no Anne. But in the front pew sat Kimberly with a smile on her face.

Lord, I only have a week to tell Kimberly what I want to do. I can't make this decision without Your help. Tell me what it is You want me to do.

"Go before you miss his sermon," Leah said, shooing Anne out the door.

Anne leaned over the ledge of the half door into the toddler's room. "Are you sure you can handle this by yourself?"

"Yes. We only have eight children and you weren't supposed to work the late service anyway."

"But your help didn't show up."

"Yeah, Gina got sick. That happens. I've learned to adjust to life's little surprises. Now go." Leah waved her hand toward the nave.

As Anne neared the place of worship, her palms became sweaty, her heartbeat accelerated. She didn't have a right to enter the sanctuary. Confusion made her steps leaden. With trembling hands she opened one of the double doors and slipped into the church.

Spotting a seat at the back, Anne took it as Caleb stood up and walked to the front of the altar area and faced his parishioners. He paused, scanning the crowd. When his gaze lit upon her, his whole face brightened with a smile that deeply creased the corner of his eyes. He nodded his head toward her, then began his sermon, his rich baritone voice ringing out.

As he spoke, his words snuck into her mind and stayed, planting themselves deep into her thoughts. His sermon was simply about love: love for God, love for yourself, love for others.

Caleb moved closer to the front pew. "Hear the words from John, 'And we have known and believed the love that God hath to us. God is love; and he that dwelleth in love dwelleth in God, and God in him.' Without God or love, our lives are not rich and full. They go hand in hand to guarantee us happiness."

Love. God. Was it that simple? Just believe in God and give Him your love and He will return it? Anne had never really had that in her life. Her parents hadn't loved her, only tolerated her as their daughter.

"And remember what Proverbs said, 'I love them that love Me, and those that seek Me early shall find Me.' Take that with you into the work week and glorify your love for the Lord Jesus Christ in all that you do. Now let us pray." Caleb bowed his head.

Folding her clasped hands in her lap, Anne followed suit. All she had to do was reach out to God and He would embrace her? She had no reference in her life for that kind of unconditional love.

Was it really that simple?

When the service was over, Anne sought to escape before Caleb found her. She had much to think over. But she only got as far as the double doors that led to the foyer.

A hand grasped her arm, halting her progress.

"Anne, I'm so glad you could make it."

She stepped to the side to allow others to pass her and Caleb. "I said I would. It was a thought-provoking sermon."

"Then I've done what I set out to do, stir people's thoughts about God. Do you have a moment? There's someone I would like you to meet."

Anne peered down the hallway that led to the classrooms. "I wanted to see if Leah needed any help cleaning up."

"Go. I'll bring Kimberly to the classroom."

As Anne walked away, she felt Caleb's gaze on her back, boring a hole through her. Kimberly. His friend from Africa. Or was she going to be more than a friend? That question plagued Anne the whole time she assisted Leah in picking up the toys and washing down the tables where the children had glued colorful fall leaves on paper in a collage.

"Thanks for coming back, Anne, but you didn't have to." Leah put away the last of the books onto the shelf where they were stored.

"It's much easier if there are two of us cleaning up." Besides, it kept her hands busy while her mind raced with the thought of meeting—her rival for Caleb.

"I'll see you next Sunday." Leah left the room.

Anne started for the door to leave, too, when Caleb, accompanied by a beautiful woman, appeared in the doorway. At the sight of Kimberly Forrester up close, Anne's stomach lurched. Tall and slender, with very long dark brown hair, green eyes that sparkled like gems and pouty lips, Kimberly made Anne feel unattractive. She put a halt to those thoughts. According to Caleb, everyone was beautiful in God's eyes. She had a lot to offer and it was time she remembered that.

Anne extended her hand. "You must be Kimberly. It's nice to meet you."

"Likewise."

"We're going to see Dylan. Would you like a ride, Anne?"

It was one thing to be developing a positive self-image and starting to feel good about herself, but Anne wasn't going to test that by being a third wheel with Caleb and Kimberly. She shook her head. "I'm going later after brunch with Pilar, Meg and Rachel."

"Then you aren't coming to the meeting at the center today?" Caleb asked.

"No, I can't. After I see Dylan, I've got to catch up on some work at Tiny Blessings. I have missed so much it has piled up on my desk. Kelly's patience will only go so far."

"I understand." Caleb moved toward the door.

Anne watched them leave, wondering if Caleb really understood. Because she didn't. She should be fighting for him, and yet she didn't know how to go about doing that. She'd rarely dated and certainly hadn't had a serious relationship with any man.

Anne sank into a rocking chair and sighed.

God, what do I do? Are You for real? Please help me to see You, to know the kind of unconditional love You talk about. Please help me to turn over control to You.

"Anne's pretty," Kimberly said, breaking the silence that had fallen between them on the ride into Richmond.

Caleb glanced at Kimberly as he turned into the parking lot at the hospital. "Yes, she is. A very caring person."

"Are you in love with her? Is she the reason you haven't given me an answer?"

"Yes and no. I have more than Anne to consider. I have obligations at the youth center, too."

"I'm sure you're excellent with the children, but not many people can really handle the job required starting a mission in a remote part of the world. You can."

"I appreciate the vote of confidence but—"

"Caleb," Kimberly interrupted. "Is the idea of marrying me what's stopping you from going? Because if so, we don't have to get married. I just remembered the talks about the future we used to have after a long, hard day. I didn't mean to be so bold and overstep my bounds. I don't want that to be the reason. You belong in Africa."

Parking, Caleb angled around to face her. "And I belong in Chestnut Grove. Each serves God but in different ways."

"Then I will pray that you find an answer."

"Thank you. I will, too."

In the hospital Caleb rode the elevator up to the floor where Dylan was now staying after being taken out of ICU. As he approached the room, a tightness about his chest squeezed his lungs. He drew in a deep breath, then another.

As he passed the nurses' station, one of the nurses said, "Reverend Williams, Dylan woke up an hour ago. We tried calling you and left a message on your cell phone."

Caleb stopped in his tracks. He had turned his phone off during Sunday service and had forgotten to switch it back on. "How is he?" The pressure in his chest expanded. *Please let him be okay, Lord.*

"He's doing fine. He wanted some cake to eat with his lunch."

Caleb smiled and hurried toward Dylan's room with Kimberly trying to keep up with his long strides.

Inside he spied Dylan clicking the remote on his television set. "Well, it's about time you woke up."

Dylan swung his attention toward the door

and grinned. "They said you'd been here every day. You and Anne. Where is she?" The boy's gaze settled on Kimberly and he frowned. "Who are you?"

"Kimberly. I'm a friend of Caleb's from Africa."

"Africa. Have you seen lions and elephants?"

"Yes, many times, as well as other animals like hippos, rhinos, cheetahs, gorillas."

"Man! That would be cool to see. I wish I could go to Africa one day."

"Maybe you'll get to," Caleb said, pulling up two chairs for himself and Kimberly.

"Where's Anne?"

"She'll be here later. She had to meet with some people and was coming right after that. You gave us a fright, you know."

"The nurses said my dad didn't come to the hospital. Is he all right?"

"He's fine, only a few bruises. But the police are charging with him drunk driving. I understand this wasn't his first offense."

Dylan's head dropped and he stared at his lap. "No. I shouldn't have asked him to pick me up." He grasped some of his top sheet and crushed it in his hand. Looking at Caleb again, he asked, "My dad is never gonna change, is he?"

"I can't answer that for sure. I suspect he won't unless something drastic changes in his life. I will tell you, Dylan, that your father has decided to give you up for adoption. He loves you enough to realize he can't give you what you need. He wants you to have a stable, loving home to live in."

The child's eyes filled with tears. "He does?"

"Yes. I don't think that decision came easily for him. But he saw what happened with the accident and that you almost died. He's protecting you."

The tears spilled out and flowed down Dylan's cheeks. "But I don't have anywhere to go. I don't want to live at the Givens' house. They don't care about me."

Seeing Dylan's pain cemented in Caleb's mind what he needed to do. *Lord, thank You for showing me the way.* "What if you move to Reverend Fraser's house until I've been approved to be a foster parent? The Frasers would love to have you until I can. I'm looking for a better place so you'll have your own bedroom. And if you agree, I would like to adopt you."

Dylan's mouth fell open, then the biggest grin appeared on his face. "Yes!"

"You realize this all will take some time.

Are you willing to stick around long enough to become my son?"

Even though Dylan was smiling, his eyes glistened with renewed tears. "Yes!"

Kimberly settled her hand on Caleb's shoulder. "You two will make a dynamite family."

Caleb stayed for another hour before he had to leave to get back to Chestnut Grove for his Sunday afternoon meeting at the youth center.

The second he was behind the wheel Kimberly said, "I've got my answer. I figured you'd be staying."

"Yes. This is where I belong."

"What about Anne? Do you have plans to be with her?"

The joy of the past hour vanished. "Anne isn't a Christian."

"But she was at the church today."

"She's been exploring our faith, but I need to cut my losses before I get hurt like before."

"Ah, you mean your ex-fiancée?"

"Yep. I don't want to go through that again. It didn't work when I tried to convert her and I ended up devastated."

"But Anne isn't her. Is that the real reason or are you scared to make that kind of commitment because you were burned once?"

Caleb didn't have an answer for Kimberly. Being the good friend she was, she knew all about his past relationships and he knew about hers. They had shared everything while living and working in Africa. Why hadn't he fallen in love with her instead of Anne? Everything would have been much simpler.

Driving by the youth center, Anne almost stopped to see Caleb. But she knew he was in the middle of his Sunday afternoon meeting with the kids and she didn't want to disturb him. Okay, she was afraid to see him again.

According to Dylan, Caleb had been with Kimberly today at the hospital—which she knew—but the child had gone on and on about how neat it was that Kimberly lived in Africa and saw wild animals every day. The only wild animals she saw every day were the squirrels and birds, which she didn't think Dylan would get too excited about.

Anne, let's face it. You're jealous of Kimberly and the relationship she'd had with Caleb over the years.

She didn't like these feelings, hadn't dealt with them before because she'd never been in love before. She'd admired a couple of men from afar, but that was as far as it had gone.

She needed to concentrate on something other than Caleb who was becoming more and more unattainable. Dylan. Ah, now that was something to celebrate. He was awake and chattering a mile a minute, which thrilled her.

All he could talk about besides Kimberly and the wild animals was the fact that Caleb was going to adopt him. She hadn't realized, until the boy had said that, how much she had wanted to be Dylan's mother. She hadn't gotten as far as thinking about adopting him like Caleb, but she would have. She felt a bond with the child that went deep.

Now what should she do? Ask for visitation rights? She laughed at that thought even though there really wasn't anything funny about her situation.

She would never deny Caleb a chance to be Dylan's father, not that she could. Caleb deserved to make a family with Dylan. He would be a wonderful father. But what if he adopted Dylan and they both moved to Africa? How would she deal with that?

As Anne drove into the parking lot of Tiny Blessings, she thought about her dream—she and Caleb with two children and Dylan revisiting Williamsburg on a family outing. Sadness jammed her throat, threatening to evoke tears. She was not going to cry. She had to get on with her life.

Climbing from her Chevy, Anne headed to the front door of the adoption agency and unlocked it. She had tons of work to catch up on and now that Dylan was going to be all right she needed to concentrate on her job. She had a life to plan. No more plain Jane. No more being too timid and shy. She wouldn't be making speeches on stage in front of an audience any time soon, but she intended to become more openly involved in the town, maybe even enter her paintings in the annual art contest at the fair in the spring. Perhaps she'd be discovered and become a famous artist.

The world was waiting for her. She kept saying that in her mind as she made her way to her office and began working through the pile of papers on her desk.

Several hours later she thought she heard something. Pushing back her chair, she stood, walked to the entrance into her office and listened. Quiet greeted her. She strode to the front door and checked to make sure she had relocked it. She had.

Back at her office she stuck her head out into the hall and listened again. Nothing. Sighing, she renewed working, deciding her imagination was playing tricks on her, or perhaps Midnight, the resident cat, was making his rounds.

Concentrating so hard, she jumped out of her chair when the phone rang fifteen minutes later. Heart pounding, she answered it with a breathless whisper. "Hello?"

"Anne, this is Caleb."

She'd know his voice anywhere.

"I'm standing outside Tiny Blessings and the door is locked. I wanted to see you."

He did? "Okay. I'll be there in a second to unlock the door."

When she let him into the agency, his serious expression didn't calm her fast heartbeat. It sounded in her ears like thunder right before a storm struck. She waved him toward the only other chair in her office beside the one behind her desk.

"What brings you by here on a Sunday?" Such politeness, Anne thought, marveling at her level voice.

He sat. "I felt we should talk about the choices I needed to make."

"Dylan told me about you wanting to adopt him. He's so excited. I haven't seen him smile that big—ever."

Caleb grinned. "You know, I hadn't thought about it until I said it. I was talking to Dylan about his father giving him up to be adopted and the words just came out of my mouth." He shifted, kneading the back of his neck. "The thing is, it felt so right once I said it. I want to be his father."

"You'll make a good one. Dylan's lucky." Anne thought of her own father and what she had missed growing up, which was even more evident when she considered how wonderful Caleb would be. She sat back, trying to relax, but her muscles were tense. So much for being nonchalant. After drawing in a deep breath and releasing it between pursed lips, she asked, "So will you two be going to Africa after the adoption is final?"

Caleb's blue eyes grew round. "Whoa. Isn't that jumping the gun? First, I have to be awarded guardianship of Dylan. Second, I've already told Kimberly I wouldn't be taking her up on her offer."

Anne sagged back against her chair, as if her muscles had suddenly liquified. "You did?"

"Yes. It'll be a while before the adoption will go through. Kimberly needs someone—"

Crash!

Anne shot up out of her chair at the same time Caleb did. They both looked toward the doorway.

"What was that?" Anne whispered, tension whipping down her length.

"I don't know. You stay here while I go take a look. Is someone else working this evening?"

Anne shook her head, then realized that Caleb couldn't see her answer because he was already heading toward the hallway. "No, I don't think so. I didn't check, though, when I came in. Maybe Midnight knocked something over. He likes to get up on the top of things." She'd forgotten about the cat that Kelly had taken in and kept at the agency. Midnight occasionally caught mice, which insured him having a home since none of them like to have a mouse running around. "There's a cat door he uses to come and go as he pleases." She came up behind him.

He pivoted toward her. "What do you think you're doing? Stay here."

"But—"

"No, buts, Anne. I'm sure it's Midnight, but just in case…" He let his words trail off into silence as he disappeared around the doorjamb.

Anne grabbed for him to stop him, but her hand snatched thin air. She peeked into the hall, and he shook his head at her.

She popped back into her room, crossing her arms over her chest. "Men!"

Now that she thought about it, she was sure it was Midnight prowling the empty place. But she let Caleb play hero and check it out. She wasn't really in any hurry to hear what he had to say to her.

Caleb walked quietly down the long corridor, carefully checking each room as he went, trying to ignore his pulse roaring in his ears. When he arrived at Kelly's office near the front of the building, the door was closed—the only one in the hallway shut. He turned the knob slowly and eased the door open, peering inside.

Sitting on top of a filing cabinet was a black cat curled into a ball. Relief washed through him. He pushed the door completely open and stepped into the room. "So it was you, Midnight, after all." He started toward the cat when he suddenly wondered how in the world the cat had gotten into a closed office. He halted and began to pivot.

Out of the corner of his eye, he saw something dark coming at him. He moved back, but a solid object crashed into the side of his head, sending him spiraling down. Anne. He couldn't lose consciousness. He had to save Anne from the intruder.

His body hit the floor and his world spun

even more. He reached out at a brown clad leg, grasping cotton material for a few seconds before it was jerked from his slack grip.

Another blow sent him into the darkness…

Chapter Twelve

Anne stared at the second hand on her watch. Where was Caleb? He should have been back by now. Chilled, she rubbed her hands up and down her arms.

The sound of a door slamming coming from the back sent Anne out into the hallway. She caught a glimpse of someone dressed all in dark brown fleeing.

Caleb!

Anne ran down the corridor, checking each room. When she reached Kelly's office, she saw Caleb lying on the floor, face down, blood pooling on the floor beneath his head.

No! Her heart wrenching, she scrambled forward, kneeling to check his pulse. She'd never been more relieved than when she discovered that he was alive.

Before assessing his injuries, Anne grabbed the phone and punched in 911. After telling the operator what was wrong and where she was, she went back to Caleb on the floor to see where he was hurt.

"Caleb, do you hear me? You're not going to die. I won't let you. I love you too much for that."

She ran her fingers over his head and felt two gashes. When she drew her hand back, it was covered in his blood. Bile rose into her throat.

"Meow."

Anne glanced up to see Midnight stand on top of the file cabinet and stretch, then he jumped down and scurried from the office. She had a strange feeling that the cat might have been the only witness to what had occurred in this office.

Afraid to move him in case Caleb was injured some place she couldn't see, she left him on his stomach with his face turned toward her. She quickly inspected the rest of him to make sure his head wounds were the only thing wrong with him. She thought about what Dylan had just gone through and the seriousness of head injuries and shuddered.

Please, Lord, spare Caleb. He has so much more to do in this world. Save and protect him. I beg You.

The prayer came easily and naturally to her. As she waited for the ambulance and police, she said to Caleb over and over, "God will protect you. He is with you."

When she heard the pounding on the front door, she said, "I'll be right back, Caleb." She hoped somehow he could hear her talking to him.

She ran to the door and turned the lock, then stepped back to allow the paramedics in with the gurney. "He's in there." Anne pointed toward Kelly's office.

As the two men headed down the hall, Anne saw Zach's car pull up. She waited for him, her glance straying toward Kelly's office several times.

"I was at the station when your call came in. I told them I would take this. What happened?" Zach asked the second he was inside the building.

Anne made her way toward where Caleb was, anxious to see what the paramedics had to say before they transported him and hoping that Caleb had awakened during the two minutes she had been gone. When she stepped into the room, the two men were lifting him onto the gurney. His eyes were still closed and Anne got a good look at his face. There was a pasty cast to his skin that frightened her, reminding her so much of how Dylan had looked when he had been in a coma.

"How is he?" she asked, her voice shaky, her hands trembling.

"He's got a nasty gash on the side of his head and another one at the back that isn't as deep. Are you following us to the hospital, ma'am?"

"Yes. Bon Secours Richmond Community Hospital?"

"Yes, ma'am. They need information on him at the hospital."

"I'll be there. He's Caleb Williams."

"Right after she talks to me," Zach said, removing a pad and pen from his coat pocket. Then when he saw her frown, he added, "It won't take long, Anne. I promise. I'm calling Pilar to take you to the hospital. I don't want you driving by yourself."

"I can drive myself. I'm not going to fall apart."

She moved out of the way of the paramedics as they rolled Caleb out of the office. Watching him leave stole what composure she had. She sank onto a chair by the desk, her legs quivering. The trembling spread to encompass her whole body, momentarily making a mockery of her declaration.

"You have to catch whoever did this to him," Anne whispered to Zach.

He walked around the room, checking the area and taking a few notes while Anne gathered her poise about her and prepared herself to answer his questions. She was strong. Caleb needed her.

"What happened?"

"I'm really not sure. We heard a noise and thought it was the cat. Caleb came to check. When he didn't come back and I heard the back door slamming, I went out into the hall to check on him. Through the window beside the door I saw someone fleeing. I found him on the floor, bleeding, and called 911."

"Could you identify the person running away?"

She shook her head. "All I saw was his back. He was wearing dark brown from head to toe."

"He?"

"I guess so. I don't know really."

"Height, weight, anything else?"

"Maybe five feet—eight, nine or ten inches." Her voice rose in frustration. "It was hard to tell. Honestly, I was only thinking about Caleb."

Zach put a hand on her shoulder. "I know, Anne. Maybe when Caleb wakes up he can tell us who did this. In the meantime, I'll get a team out here to go over the place. First the fire and now this break-in. Something's going on, all right."

Anne rose. "Can I leave now?"

"Yes. I'll call Pilar. She can at least meet you there. I'll come by later and see how Caleb is."

Anne hurried from the room, not wanting to stay another second. The office sent chills down her spine. What if Caleb went into a coma and never regained consciousness? That had been a very real possibility with Dylan. Her whole body shook with a bone-deep cold.

On the drive to the hospital Anne murmured a prayer to God to be with Caleb and protect him. She was so afraid she would never see him smile again—or, for that matter, frown.

Parking near the emergency entrance, she was out of her car and running toward the doors. When she entered, she went directly to the desk to ask about him. The nurse told her to sit in the waiting room because the doctors were examining him at the moment. Before Anne left the desk, she gave the woman what information she could about Caleb. Then she took up her vigil in the waiting room, so reminiscent of only the week before when she had been in the very same place waiting to hear news about Dylan.

Fifteen minutes later Pilar came into the room and Anne sagged with relief to have a friend with her. She had felt so alone. She stood and hugged Pilar, tears rushing to the surface and flowing down Anne's cheeks.

"Oh, Anne, I'm so sorry. Have they said anything about Caleb yet?"

"No. This waiting is killing me! I keep thinking the worst. Pilar, I love him. I don't want him to die."

Her friend took her hands and sat. "He's not going to die."

"You didn't see the wounds, his face when they took him away. He was unconscious. From Dylan, I know how tricky head injuries can be. I—" Her mind refused to think beyond that.

"Then you know, like Dylan, he can wake up at any moment and be fine."

Anne nodded and latched onto that hope. "Yes, you're right."

"Zach will find out who did this to Caleb."

A few minutes later a woman doctor entered and found Anne. "Mr. Williams is being admitted to the hospital. He hasn't regained consciousness yet. He's got a concussion that will have to be watched."

Anne pushed to her feet. "Can I see him?"

"He'll be in a room in half an hour. We're running some tests on him first."

After the doctor left, Pilar said, "Let's get something to drink to help us stay awake."

"I need to do something first. I'll meet you in the cafeteria." Anne didn't wait for her friend's reply. She strode from the room, a need to go to the chapel overpowering.

Inside the chapel she sat and bowed her head. "Lord, I'm here to ask You to save Caleb. I know I haven't done much praying, in fact none, until recently, but I need Your help. Caleb needs Your help. He's a good man who has so much still to do. Dylan is depending on him. Please don't take him away if for no one's sake but Dylan's. Grandma Rose and Caleb have always believed in You and Your power. I don't want anything for myself. Just Caleb."

She lifted her head toward the simple altar and felt a peace come over her that she had never experienced before. Stunned, she stared at the altar, her arms going limp at her side. God was with her. More importantly God was with Caleb. He would be all right.

* * *

Anne sat on the small couch in Caleb's hospital room with Pilar next to her. Anne drank her hot tea while her friend sipped her coffee. It had been four hours since he had been brought into the room and the time had flown by with Pilar. Anne had so many questions she wanted answered concerning the Lord and her friend had been most accommodating.

"You should go home now, Pilar. You don't need to stay with me any longer. It's nearly midnight."

"You should get some rest, too."

"I'm not leaving this place until Caleb wakes up and tells me to go home and sleep."

"Does he know how you feel about Jesus?"

"No, and I don't want you telling him anything." Anne finished her tea and crushed the paper cup into a ball.

"I won't, but you should."

"I will when the time is right. It's all so new to me. When Dylan was in the hospital, I accused God of a lot of things. I was wrong. Caleb kept telling me the Lord had plans for us that weren't always obvious to us at first. With Dylan I see that now. The accident opened the way for Caleb to adopt Dylan. He will be so much better with Caleb as his father and God knew that."

"I find a crisis can either strengthen a person's belief or weaken it, sometimes destroy it. I like your positive thinking about Caleb's recovery."

"He *will* recover." Anne laid her hand over her heart. "I know it in here."

Pilar stood and stretched. "Are you sure you don't need me?"

"I will always need your friendship, but right now I want you to go home to your husband." Anne rose and gave Pilar a hug.

After her friend left, Anne scooted a chair to Caleb's bed and took his hand. It was cool to the touch. His face still had an ashen cast to it, but she wasn't worried anymore. He was under God's protection.

"Caleb, I will be here when you wake up. I saw Dylan earlier and he will be here, too. I had to make him go back to his room. He wanted to stay. He's getting out of the hospital tomorrow. He's gonna be okay. Just like you. I love you." As before, Anne hoped he could hear her and respond to the sound of her voice. "Dear God, it's me again. Ease his pain and help him find his way back to Dylan and me."

* * *

Caleb's head pulsated with pain. But through that he thought he heard Anne talking. She was all right. Nothing happened to her. That diminished the pounding against his skull momentarily. He didn't have to worry somehow that—what? He couldn't remember.

He shifted.

"Caleb?"

Anne's voice again reached into the darkness and beckoned him toward the light. He felt the coolness of her hand wrapped around his, but the weight on his eyelids kept him from opening them.

"Caleb, I'm here for you."

Anne! He called out in his mind before the pain engulfed him in its throbbing intensity and whisked him back into the black hole.

"Pilar called us," Meg said, entering Caleb's hospital room.

Anne lifted her head that felt as though it weighed a ton. She supposed that was what going without sleep does to a person. But she was so afraid to shut her eyes just in case Caleb awakened. She attempted a smile for Meg and Rachel's benefit that she could tell hadn't worked because of their worried expressions.

"You need to go home, Anne Smith." Rachel scurried toward her as if she were going to escort her from the room right that moment.

Anne latched on to the arms of the chair she sat in beside Caleb's bed. "No. I can't leave until I know he will be all right. Do you think I could honestly sleep knowing that Caleb—" She couldn't finish her sentence. She couldn't say aloud the worse thing that could happen to Caleb, that he die. The thought sent terror screaming through her. If he died, it was God's will, but she desperately needed to tell Caleb she loved him and the Lord.

Rachel held up her hands. "Okay, then how about something to eat? You can't go without sleep and food."

"I could stand to lose a little weight," Anne quipped, this time her mouth tilting up in a half grin.

Rachel settled her balled hand on her waist. "Well, I'm going to get you something to eat whether you like it or not." She hurried out of the room before Anne could stop her.

Anne snapped her attention to Meg, who

hovered at the end of Caleb's bed. "Okay, let me hear it."

Meg quirked a brow. "Hear what?"

"Why I should leave here."

"I wouldn't dare say that to you. If Jared was here, a team of wild horses couldn't drag me away from the man I loved."

Anne dropped her head into her palms. "Does everyone know?"

"What, that Caleb is in the hospital or that you love him?"

Scrubbing her hands down her face, she looked up at her friend. "Both."

"Yep."

Oh, it was worse than she thought. What if the adoption goes through quickly? Will Caleb take Kimberley up on her offer? Will he and Dylan move to Africa, even without Kimberly? She would have to face the whole town a rejected woman again.

You are strong now, Anne. I am with you to the end of time. Those comforting words came into Anne's mind, bringing with them the peace she had experienced in the chapel. She straightened in her chair, lifted her chin and said, "I don't want a parade of visitors in here until he is better. He will need his rest."

Meg chuckled. "I like your mother-henning, if there is such a word."

"You can stay until Rachel comes back with no doubt several sacks of food for me."

"Thanks," Meg said with a bark of laughter. "I like the new you. A month ago you wouldn't have said anything like that to me."

"A month ago I wouldn't have been sitting here. Caleb and the Lord changed all that."

Meg pulled up the other chair beside Anne. "You believe?"

Anne nodded. "It's been happening for some time, but yesterday evening in the chapel, I had a conversation with our Father in Heaven and He answered me." She thumped her chest. "Me, the doubter. Caleb is going to be all right. God is repairing him as we speak." She reached out her hand. "But it wouldn't hurt for us to say another prayer for his recovery. Will you join me?"

Meg's eyes glistened. She sniffled. "Yes, I would be honored."

Her friend clasped her outstretched hand. Anne felt the strength and bond of friendship in that grasp and appreciated how fortunate she had been all these years to have not one but three best friends. She had been blessed and hadn't really realized the full extent.

Anne bowed her head. "Father, I am joined here today with my friend, Meg. We are asking for Your protection and guidance in bringing Caleb back to us whole and sound. Also, Lord, have mercy on the one who did this to Caleb. He is a troubled soul who doesn't know You. Amen."

Again Caleb heard Anne's voice through the shroud of pain that blanketed his mind. Its musical quality was a balm that touched his heart. But the words she uttered, a prayer, reached into his soul and roused him from the darkness.

His eyelids inched up, allowing a slither of light in. He winced and immediately closed them. Pain, caused by the brightness, pierced his skull, and he groaned.

"Caleb?"

Anne hovered over him. He could smell her apple-scented shampoo.

"Meg, he moved. I saw it! Did you see it?"

"No, but I wasn't looking."

"Caleb, I'm here."

His mouth felt as though cotton had been rammed down his throat. He swallowed and murmured, "An-ne."

She touched him. "I'm here."

"Lig-light."

"It's too bright in here," he heard Anne say. "Meg, please close the blinds."

The sound of the blinds closing prompted him to try again. He eased his eyes open a slit and saw Anne's beautiful face in the dimness above him. He wanted to smile, but his mouth wouldn't cooperate.

Instead he whispered in a raw voice, "Hi."

"Hi, yourself." Anne leaned down. "I know you've been tired lately, but is this any way to get extra rest?"

In his mind he laughed. "Fun-ny."

"I'll go tell the nurse that Caleb is awake," Meg said behind Anne.

Light poured into the room when Meg opened the door. He flinched away and the pain in his head magnified by the sudden movement.

"I'm not even going to ask how you feel. I can tell by the way you look. Just believe me, it will get better."

"I do." He slid his glance toward the bedside table. "Water."

"Oh, of course. Let me raise the bed so you can have a drink."

After she adjusted the bed, Anne held the plastic cup to his lips and the coolness alleviated some of the dryness in his mouth and throat.

When she put the cup back on the table, Caleb asked, "What happened?"

Anne told him about the events that led up to him being in the hospital. "Do you remember any of this?"

"I remember going down the hall. Seeing the cat. Then nothing."

"That's understandable. You were hit twice on the head."

He started to touch his head, then thought about it and decided that wouldn't be wise. "So that accounts for the elephants tap-dancing on my brain."

"You can always count on elephants to be heavy-footed."

Caleb grinned, then groaned. "Please, Anne, don't make me laugh. It hurts too much."

Concern chased away the smile on her face. "I'm sorry. I—"

He reached for her hand. "No, never be sorry for making a person happy with laughter. I'll just do it in my mind for the time being."

The door swished open and the doctor entered.

"It's good to see you awake, Mr. Williams. Those are two nasty bumps you have." He peered toward Anne. "May we have a moment alone while I check him over?"

"I'll be outside."

Caleb watched Anne leaving. He had so many questions to ask her. The first being: was that you I heard praying to God?

"What are you two doing out in the hall?" Rachel asked, clutching two small sacks.

"Caleb is awake and the doctor is checking him out," Meg answered.

The scent of French fries tantalized Anne's hunger. Now that Caleb was awake she was starved. Grabbing for the bag Rachel held out, Anne opened it and drew in a deep breath. "I know fries aren't nutritious, but they smell wonderful to a famished person."

"I wasn't exactly sure what you would eat so I brought you a little of everything." Rachel thrust the second sack into her hands. "*Bon appetit.*"

"Thanks, both of you." Anne popped a fry into her mouth and savored the greasy, salty taste.

"We've got to go." Meg took hold of Rachel's arm.

"I just got here. I wanted to say hi to Caleb."

"Later." Meg motioned for Rachel to walk toward the elevator.

Anne laughed at the pair and dug into the bag for several more fries. She saw Meg whisper something to Rachel, then her friend glanced back at her and smiled.

"We'll stop by tomorrow," Rachel said, winking.

As the elevator doors shut on her best friends, the doctor came out of the room. He hurried down the hall.

Anne went after him and planted herself in front of the man. "Will he be okay?" When she had time later to think about what she had done, she was sure she would be amazed. She never chased people down to get some information.

"I'm keeping him here another day to be on the safe side, but I see no reason that he won't fully recover."

Anne smiled. "Thank you." She strode back toward Caleb's room, whispering, "And thank You, God."

When she entered, Caleb's eyes were closed, but he immediately opened them and grinned. "What took you so long?"

She sat again in the chair by his bed. "Just checking with your doctor." She stuck her hand into the sack and dragged out more fries. "Want any?"

"No, my stomach is a little queasy from the medication. But please go ahead and eat. Then we can talk."

Her hunger vanished with those words. "Talk?"

"I do remember we were in the middle of a conversation when we were interrupted."

Anne gulped, her insecurities nibbling at her composure. No, she wouldn't allow them to dominate her life as they had in the past. "Okay. Let's talk." She rolled up the bags and set them on the floor by her chair.

He looked down at the sacks. "But—"

"I'm not that hungry and this is important."

The sound of the door opening brought a moan to Anne's lips. Then she saw Dylan being wheeled into the room, and she smiled at the young boy.

"The nurse said you were awake. It's about time." Dylan glanced back at the young woman who had brought him and said, "Thanks." When she left, he continued, "I'm getting out of here today. How about you?"

"The doc says another day."

"Aw, man, I was hoping we could leave together."

"It'll take a little time, but we'll be together soon."

"Promise?" Dylan rolled himself closer to the bed.

"Yep." Caleb's gaze sought Anne's. "I suspect in the next few months my life is gonna change a lot."

"Change is good," Anne said.

Caleb nodded, then winced at the movement of his head, bringing his hand up to massage his temple.

"Do you want me to see if they can give you anything more for the pain?" Anne hated seeing him hurting.

"The doctor gave me some Tylenol."

Looking at the pain etched into his features, she asked, "Nothing stronger?"

"Can't have anything stronger. They're going to keep a close watch on me for the next twenty-four hours to make sure I don't have any neurological problems. Anything stronger will mask those problems." He shifted his gaze to Dylan. "I'll have to be tough for the time being. So have you been doing any wheelies in that wheelchair?"

Dylan laughed. "They won't let me. I'm gonna have to use crutches when I get out of here."

"I had to once when I hurt my ankle playing soccer." Caleb dropped his hand back to his side.

"You played soccer? For long?"

"Nope. That injury ended my short-lived career. I had visions of going to the Olympics."

The door opened again. Anne shook her head and said, "I believe this is Grand Central Station."

Ross Van Zandt, a private investigator Anne had met before, entered the room. He looked as though he had been up all night as he had a bit of a stubble, his dark hair was tousled, and his dark eyes were somber, tired. "I'm glad to see you're better. Can you answer a few questions for me?"

Caleb frowned. "I don't think I can help you. I—"

The swishing sound of the door cut off Caleb's words. Everyone turned to see who was coming into the room this time.

Anne sagged back against the chair. "Zach, you too? I wonder who's gonna be next."

Zach scanned the faces of the people all around Caleb's bed. When his gaze settled on Anne, he said, "Meg called Pilar, who called me at the station and told me Caleb finally woke up." Then to Caleb he said, "I have some questions for you."

Anne rose. "Dylan, I think that's our cue to leave."

"Aw, do we have to? This is getting good."

Anne gripped the back of the wheelchair and rolled the boy toward the door, which Ross held open. "Don't you have some packing to do, young man?"

"Packing? I don't have anything at the hospital except the clothes Mr. Givens brought me to wear out of here."

"How about all those gifts people have been bringing you?"

"Oh, I forgot about those."

The door to the room closed, and Caleb could only hear muffled voices. He turned his attention to the two men standing at the end of his bed, one a friend and the other a stranger who had come to town recently to look into something connected with the adoption agency.

Zach swung his intense regard toward Ross. "Why are you here, Van Zandt?"

"The same as you. I have questions about the break-in."

With his head throbbing and exhaustion threatening to overwhelm him, Caleb said, "Zach, if you don't mind, I'd like Ross to stay so I don't have to answer the same questions twice. It's been a horrendous twenty-four hours." He glanced at the door, wondering when Anne would come back. He had so much to tell her.

Zach harumphed. "What happened, Caleb, at the agency?"

Caleb told him about going into Kelly's office and finding the cat. "I sensed someone behind me and turned. Before I could see who it was, I was hit on the head and went down. The person struck me again, then I vaguely remember hearing running footsteps. That's all."

"Nothing about the person? Height? Gender? Any scents? Any unusual sounds?" Zach stuffed his hand into his pocket, frustration evident in his expression.

"Sorry. It happened so fast. I just don't remember anything more than what I told you. I know it isn't much."

One corner of Zach's mouth quirked up. "You know where you can reach me if you remember anything at all. Even the smallest detail can be important."

"Sure. You'll be the first to know." He closed his eyes for a few seconds, the past hour or so a whirlwind spinning around inside his mind, escalating his weariness.

"We're going," Zach said, seeing his friend's pale, drawn features. "I'm glad you're all right. Van Zandt, you coming?" He tossed his head toward the door.

Out in the corridor Zach rounded on Van

Zandt. "Why are you interested in the break-in? Who are you working for?"

"You know I can't tell you that. My client doesn't want people to know. I can tell you I'm looking for a biological mother's adult child, which is the reason I'm interested in anything having to do with the adoption agency."

"You think there's a connection between the break-in and this child or mother?"

"Don't know. That's why I'm asking questions." Ross rubbed his hand over the stubble on his jaw. "If you don't need to ask me any more questions, I'm heading back to Chestnut Grove."

Zach observed the man he knew once had been a cop walk toward the elevator. Had the woman Van Zandt worked for gone as far as breaking into the adoption agency to find her child? Would she ransack Kelly's office looking for that information? Or was something else going on here?

When Anne returned to Caleb's room, she found him asleep. She took up her post in the chair next to his bed and waited for him to wake up. Part of her dreaded their conversation to come, part of her wanted it immediately.

The nurse came into the room. "How long has he been asleep?"

"Not long. Maybe thirty minutes."

"I hate doing this, but I need to wake him up. I'll have to do it every two hours and check some things."

"Do you need me to leave?"

"No," the older woman said and shook Caleb's shoulder.

Caleb's eyes slowly inched open. A question was in his gaze when he looked at the nurse, then he saw Anne and smiled, his whole attention focused on her.

"I'm going to shine this light in your eyes." The nurse stepped up to the other side of the bed.

After she performed that task, she had Caleb grasp her fingers and squeeze as tight as he could. "Can you touch your right forefinger to your nose? Now, your left forefinger. Wiggle your toes. Good."

When she finished and left, Caleb chuckled. "I felt like I was playing Simon Says. I must have passed the test. That's a relief. I don't like failing. Mom always said I was an overachiever."

"I was an underachiever. I didn't want to draw attention to myself."

Caleb shifted on the bed, being careful not to move too suddenly. "Maybe we can talk now."

"If you don't have any more visitors."

"Then I'd better be quick about it." He reached for her hand and clasped it. "Anne, I heard you praying earlier with Meg. In fact, I think I heard you praying several times since the accident, either that or I was dreaming."

"No, I prayed all night and morning long. You weren't dreaming."

"You believe in God?"

Her throat swelling with emotions, she nodded.

"When? What happened?"

"I think it's been happening for some time. I have seen how devoted Meg, Pilar and Rachel are and wondered about it. I would ask them questions. Then I got to know you better and memories of my time with Grandma Rose surfaced. Those were the best times of my life. She was a strong believer and tried to convince me when I was a little girl. But then I would go home to my father and mother who don't believe and I wouldn't do any further exploration. In fact, they discouraged me if I ever asked them about God."

"It's hard when a child doesn't have the proper foundation."

Anne perched on the edge of the chair, excitement bubbling inside her. "After you arrived at the hospital, I went to the chapel to have a heart-to-heart with God. I walked into that room, confused, worried. I walked out, knowing that you would be all right in the Lord's hands. I've never felt that way in all my whole twenty-nine years. I want more of that feeling."

"Isn't it wonderful? There isn't a better feeling in the world than to know God is always with you, watching over you."

"We are not alone."

"Exactly. Come here." He patted the side of the bed while he scooted over to give her room to sit. Lifting his hand, he cupped her head. "I love you, Anne. I want to marry you. I want us, you, me and Dylan, to be a family. Will you marry me?"

She leaned down and feathered her lips across his, drinking in the sight of him. "Yes. When you were talking to Dylan, I was jealous that I wasn't included in those plans."

His hand cradling her head brought her close so he could sample her lips again. Deepening the kiss, he plunged his fingers into her hair. "You don't ever have to be jealous again. What Dylan really needs is not only a father, but a mother as well."

"How about sisters and brothers?"

An impish gleam sparkled in his blue eyes. "That, too."

"Mr. Williams, I like the way you think."

Epilogue

"Being in love becomes you," Meg said as she slipped into the booth at the Starlight Diner next to Anne.

"Is it the constant smile on my face or the glow about me that gives my secret away?" Anne opened the menu she knew by heart. On Sunday her order had never varied—a bacon cheeseburger.

"Secret!" Rachel exclaimed. "That glow about you could light the whole town. Everyone in Chestnut Grove is talking about you and Caleb getting married."

Pilar hurried over to the table. "Sorry I'm late. Reverend Fraser needed to speak to me after church. Did I miss anything?"

"We were discussing Anne being in love."

Rachel scooted over to allow Pilar to sit in the booth.

"What I want to know is have you two set a date yet for the big event?" Meg asked.

Anne leaned forward, drawing her friends closer. "New Year's Eve. Isn't that romantic? Caleb came up with that date. He doesn't want to wait any longer."

"What a great way to celebrate the New Year with the beginning of your marriage."

Sandra came over to take their orders and put tall glasses of ice water on the table. "Congratulations, Anne. Caleb's a wonderful man."

Anne beamed. "Yes, I totally agree. How are you feeling?"

"I'm doing okay. There are some days that are better than others, but thank the Lord I am here to enjoy the day."

After Sandra left, Rachel lifted her glass and said, "To Anne and Caleb. The last of our little group to get married."

Anne clicked her glass against the others. "This has been a very good year for us. We've been blessed, especially me. Not only did I find love, I discovered the importance of God in my life." If only she had realized His power while she was growing up and dealing with taunts from others and the lack of acceptance from her parents, maybe then she wouldn't have withdrawn into a shell. Now, though, she had a second chance.

"Isn't love grand?" Rachel asked, lifting her water to her lips. "Now I just need to find someone for my brother-in-law. Ben and Olivia need someone to care for them."

"Does Ben feel that way?" Anne took a sip of her drink, too.

"No, but a good woman could change his mind."

Meg laughed. "You aren't going to become a matchmaker, are you, Rachel Cavanaugh?"

Rachel pressed the flat of her hand over her chest. "Who me?"

"Yeah, right." Pilar glanced toward the door. "Oh, look who's coming inside."

Anne turned in the booth and spied Dylan on crutches with Caleb making their way toward them. Her heartbeat accelerated at the sight of the man she loved, and she went all weak-kneed. Thankfully she was sitting down.

"Hi. Dylan and I thought we would grab something to eat before heading for the center."

"Yeah, and this place has the best burgers and fries," Dylan said, the cuts on his face healing nicely. "Reverend Fraser is joining us in a few minutes. I'm moving into his house later today." Dylan looked up at Caleb. "But only until Caleb gets a bigger place and the paperwork is completed for me to be with him—" the boy swung his gaze to Anne "—and you."

"We're going looking for a house this week," Anne said, sure that the smile on her face was huge, with both men in her life looking at her as though she were the most important person alive. "And we'll need your input, too, Dylan."

"Yes!" The boy pumped his free arm.

"Didn't mean to interrupt," Caleb said, leaning down and brushing his lips across Anne's before he started for a table in the back. "Get back to solving the problems of the world."

Watching them leave, Anne rested her chin in her palm and sighed.

"You're glowing," Rachel said with a laugh.

"You'll just have to get used to the new me," Anne said with a happy smile.

* * * * *

Dear Reader,

Writing the fourth book in the continuity series, TINY BLESSINGS, was an honor and a privilege. The story of Anne gaining her self-confidence through her growing faith in the Lord and her growing relationship with Caleb was a joy to write. So many times we don't always realize how unique we are as individuals and it takes someone else to point that out. Anne needed Caleb to do that for her, but he needed Anne, too. He got a second chance to share his faith with the woman he loved and to show her the power of God.

I love hearing from readers. You can contact me at P.O. Box 2074, Tulsa, OK 74101 or visit my Web site at www.margaretdaley.com where you can sign up for my quarterly newsletter.

Best wishes,

Margaret Daley

Is Leah Paxson the answer to Olivia Cavanaugh's prayers? Find out in HER CHRISTMAS WISH coming from Love Inspired in November 2005.

Chapter One

Reluctantly, Ben had to acknowledge that fact that with each passing year it had become more difficult for Nanny Baker to keep up with an active child, no matter how good-natured. And Olivia was good-natured, there was no doubt about it, but her body was as busy as her mind and her tongue had both of them beaten for speed!

When Nanny Baker had told him that her only sister in Arizona was recovering from surgery and had asked her to move in with her, he'd assumed that it would be a temporary arrangement. He'd immediately started compiling a list of *temporary* replacements until Nanny had gently corrected him. She'd been considering retirement for several months and was looking forward to being close to family again. Not, she'd quickly assured him, that he and Olivia weren't like family to her, but she knew this was something she needed to do.

Which was why they were now nannyless.

"Mr. Cavanaugh?" The director was back on the line, only now there was something new in her tone, a spark of excitement that hadn't been there before. "I was just on the telephone with Leah Paxson, one of our nannies. She was hired six months ago by a family in Richmond and she just found out the children's father has accepted a transfer to London that is effective immediately. She is returning to Chestnut Grove this afternoon and she, well she's *available*, Mr. Cavanaugh. Isn't that wonderful news!"

Ben couldn't believe it. For a moment, he didn't know what to say. The thought chased through his mind that maybe God *had* intervened, but he shook it away. He knew better.

"Did you hear me, Mr. Cavanaugh? I can set up an interview between you and Miss Paxson tomorrow."

"She's well-qualified?" Desperate circumstances or not, he wasn't going to hire just anyone to look after Olivia. He owed it to both his daughter and to the memory of his wife, Julia, to make sure that Olivia had the best of care while he was at work.

"The family asked Leah to accompany them to London," the director said. "I know they've been extremely happy with her. She's worked with our agency for five years now and I've never heard any negative comments about her. She's a natural with children."

A natural. She certainly sounded qualified. Silently, he went through his schedule for the next day and made a few adjustments.

"How does eleven o'clock tomorrow morning sound?" he asked. "I'd like her to come right to the house. My office is here and I think it would be good for her to see where she'll be living if she accepts the position."

"I'll call Miss Paxson back right away, Mr. Cavanaugh. Eleven o'clock tomorrow."

Ben hung up the phone, relief pouring through him. Mrs. Baker hadn't wanted to go to Arizona until they'd found a replacement for her, but Ben had insisted, confident that it would be a day or two at the most until Tender Care provided another nanny. He hadn't considered that a week after her departure, he'd still be waiting. And now it looked as if the wait might finally be over.

Seven years ago, he'd told Mrs. Wallace

exactly what qualifications were necessary for the woman who would be Olivia's nanny. Nanny Baker had fulfilled every one—quiet, sedate and grandmotherly. Ben could only assume that Lean Paxson would be just like her.

Leah Paxson was a firm believer in the adage, "When God closes a door, He opens a window." She reminded herself of that several times while pacing the length of her tiny studio apartment, praying about the interview that Mrs. Wallace had set up for her the following morning with Mr. Ben Cavanaugh. She was still a bit shell-shocked from the rapid change in her employment situation and although the family she'd been living with had practically begged her to go to England with them, Leah knew she had ties to the States that couldn't stretch that far.

She knew that God would direct her path, but she was still amazed at how quickly He'd answered! When she'd called Mrs. Wallace to explain what had happened, the director said she actually had a man on the other line who needed a nanny for his daughter. When she'd called back to set up the interview, all she'd told Leah was that Mr. Cavanaugh was a widower whose wife had died when his daughter was an infant. It would be a live-in position, of course, because he owned his own business and he was gone quite a bit. And the little girl—Olivia Cavanaugh—was seven.

Seven. Leah had felt a familiar but painful twist inside. Seven years ago, at the age of seventeen, Leah had given up her baby girl for adoption. After graduating from high school, she'd applied at Tender Care Childcare to be a nanny and discovered that caring for other people's children actually helped ease the ache in her heart instead of magnifying it. With every smile or hug she gave, she secretly prayed that her own child was receiving one, too, from loving parents.

"You'll let me know, won't You, God, if You want me to take this position?" Leah asked, pausing in front of the window that overlooked the street. In the years she'd worked for Tender Care, she'd always lived with the families who employed her, but she still paid rent on the studio, needing the security of knowing she had a place of her own if necessary.

Flopping down on the futon that doubled as her bed, she closed her eyes, not accustomed to the silence. The family she'd just left had had three pre-school aged children, which meant her evenings were filled with activity until that last one fell asleep. Usually by this time at night, she was tired, damp from being splashed with warm sudsy bath water nursing a sore throat from having read Dr. Seuss at leave five times. She didn't mind—it meant her arms were never empty, either.

Reaching out, Leah grabbed a pillow and hugged it against her middle. Her arms might not be empty now, but she could still feel an empty space in her heart. Maybe Olivia Cavanaugh would fill it, she thought drowsily as she fell asleep.